Winnie-the-Pooh

with
When We Were Very Young

A. A. MILNE

Illustrations by Ernest H. Shepard

Word Cloud Classics

San Diego

Canterbury Classics
An imprint of Printers Row Publishing Group
9717 Pacific Heights Blvd, San Diego, CA 92121
www.canterburyclassicsbooks.com • mail@canterburyclassicsbooks.com

Publisher: Peter Norton • Associate Publisher: Ana Parker
Art Director: Charles McStravick
Senior Developmental Editor: April Graham
Editor: Traci Douglas
Production Team: Beno Chan, Julie Greene

Cover design: Rosemary Rae
Endpapers: E. H. Shepard

Library of Congress Cataloging-in-Publication Data

Names: Milne, A. A. (Alan Alexander), 1882-1956 author. | Milne, A. A.
   (Alan Alexander), 1882-1956. Winnie-the-Pooh | Milne, A. A. (Alan
   Alexander), 1882-1956. When we were very young | Shepard, Ernest H.
   (Ernest Howard), 1879-1976 illustrator.
Title: Winnie-the-Pooh / A.A. Milne ; illustrations by Ernest H. Shepard.
Description: San Diego : Printers Row Publishing Group, [2023] | Series:
   Word cloud classics | Summary: "Includes the original text and images of
   Winnie-the-Pooh and When We Were Very Young by A. A. Milne, with
   illustrations by Ernest H. Shepard"-- Provided by publisher.
Identifiers: LCCN 2022045726 | ISBN 9781667203133 | ISBN 9781667205410
   (ebook)
Classification: LCC PR6025.I65 W645 2023 | DDC 823/.912--dc23/eng/20221219
LC record available at https://lccn.loc.gov/2022045726

Printed in Malaysia

27 26 25 24 23   1 2 3 4 5

Editor's Note: The works in this book have been published in their original form to preserve the author's intent and style.

CONTENTS

When We Were Very Young

* This poem, being in the Library of the Queen's Dolls' House, is printed here by special permission.

Winnie-the-Pooh

TO HER

HAND IN HAND WE COME
CHRISTOPHER ROBIN AND I
TO LAY THIS BOOK IN YOUR LAP.
SAY YOU'RE SURPRISED?
SAY YOU LIKE IT?
SAY IT'S JUST WHAT YOU WANTED?
BECAUSE IT'S YOURS—
BECAUSE WE LOVE YOU.

Introduction

If you happen to have read another book about Christopher Robin, you may remember that he once had a swan (or the swan had Christopher Robin, I don't know which) and that he used to call this swan Pooh. That was a long time ago, and when we said good-bye, we took the name with us, as we didn't think the swan would want it any more. Well, when Edward Bear said that he would like an exciting name all to himself, Christopher Robin said at once, without stopping to think, that he was Winnie-the-Pooh. And he was. So, as I have explained the Pooh part, I will now explain the rest of it.

You can't be in London for long without going to the Zoo. There are some people who begin the Zoo at the beginning, called WAYIN, and walk as quickly as they can past every cage until they get to the one called WAYOUT, but the nicest people go straight to the animal they love the most, and stay there. So when Christopher Robin goes to the Zoo, he goes to where the Polar Bears are, and he whispers something to the third keeper from the left, and doors are unlocked, and we wander through dark passages and up steep stairs, until at last we come to the special cage, and the cage is opened, and out trots something brown and furry, and with a happy cry of "Oh, Bear!" Christopher Robin rushes into its arms. Now this bear's name is Winnie, which shows what a good name for bears it is, but the funny thing is that we can't remember whether Winnie is called after Pooh, or Pooh after Winnie. We did know once, but we have forgotten. . . .

I had written as far as this when Piglet looked up and said in his squeaky voice, "What about *Me?*" "My dear Piglet," I said, "the whole book is about you." "So it is about Pooh," he squeaked. You see what it is. He is jealous because he thinks Pooh is having a Grand Introduction all to himself. Pooh is the favourite, of course, there's no denying it, but Piglet comes in for a good many things which Pooh misses; because you can't take Pooh to school without everybody knowing it, but Piglet is so small that he slips into a pocket, where it is very comfortable to feel him when you are not quite sure whether twice seven is twelve or twenty-two. Sometimes he slips out and has a good look in the ink-pot, and in this way he has got more education than Pooh, but Pooh doesn't mind. Some have brains, and some haven't, he says, and there it is.

And now all the others are saying, "What about *Us?*" So perhaps the best thing to do is to stop writing Introductions and get on with the book.

A. A. M.

Chapter I

In Which
We Are Introduced to Winnie-the-Pooh
and Some Bees, and the Stories Begin

Here is Edward Bear, coming downstairs now, bump, bump, bump, on the back of his head, behind Christopher Robin. It is, as far as he knows, the only way of coming downstairs, but sometimes he feels that there really is another way, if only he could stop bumping for a moment and think of it. And then he feels that perhaps there isn't. Anyhow, here he is at the bottom, and ready to be introduced to you. Winnie-the-Pooh.

When I first heard his name, I said, just as you are going to say, "But I thought he was a boy?"

"So did I," said Christopher Robin.

"Then you can't call him Winnie?"

"I don't."

"But you said—"

"He's Winnie-ther-Pooh. Don't you know what '*ther*' means?"

"Ah, yes, now I do," I said quickly; and I hope you do too, because it is all the explanation you are going to get.

Sometimes Winnie-the-Pooh likes a game of some sort when he comes downstairs, and sometimes he likes to sit quietly in front of the fire and listen to a story. This evening—

"What about a story?" said Christopher Robin.

"*What* about a story?" I said.

"Could you very sweetly tell Winnie-the-Pooh one?"

"I suppose I could," I said. "What sort of stories does he like?"

"About himself. Because he's *that* sort of Bear."

"Oh, I see."

"So could you very sweetly?"

"I'll try," I said.

So I tried.

Once upon a time, a very long time ago now, about last Friday, Winnie-the-Pooh lived in a forest all by himself under the name of Sanders.

(*"What does 'under the name' mean?" asked Christopher Robin.*

"It means he had the name over the door in gold letters, and lived under it."

"Winnie-the-Pooh wasn't quite sure," said Christopher Robin.

"Now I am," said a growly voice.

"Then I will go on," said I.)

One day when he was out walking, he came to an open place in the middle of the forest, and in the middle of this place was a large oak-tree, and, from the top of the tree, there came a loud buzzing-noise.

Winnie-the-Pooh sat down at the foot of the tree, put his head between his paws and began to think.

First of all he said to himself: "That buzzing-noise means something. You don't get a buzzing-noise like that, just buzzing and buzzing, without its meaning something. If there's a buzzing-noise, somebody's making a buzzing-noise, and the only reason for making a buzzing-noise that *I* know of is because you're a bee."

Then he thought another long time, and said: "And the only reason for being a bee that I know of is making honey."

And then he got up, and said: "And the only reason for making honey is so as *I* can eat it." So he began to climb the tree.

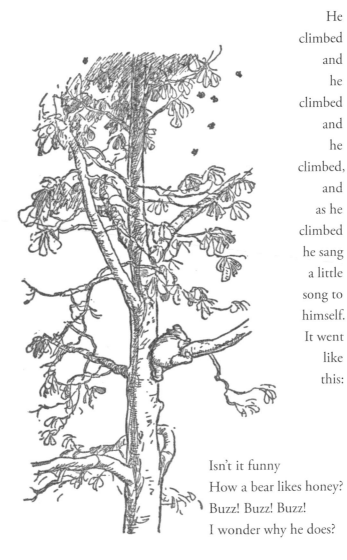

He
climbed
and
he
climbed
and
he
climbed,
and
as he
climbed
he sang
a little
song to
himself.
It went
like
this:

Isn't it funny
How a bear likes honey?
Buzz! Buzz! Buzz!
I wonder why he does?

Then he climbed a little further . . . and a little further . . . and then just a little further. By that time he had thought of another song.

> It's a very funny thought that, if Bears were Bees,
> They'd build their nests at the *bottom* of trees.
> And that being so (if the Bees were Bears),
> We shouldn't have to climb up all these stairs.

He was getting rather tired by this time, so that is why he sang a Complaining Song. He was nearly there now, and if he just stood on that branch . . .

Crack!

"Oh, help!" said Pooh, as he dropped ten feet on the branch below him.

"If only I hadn't—" he said, as he bounced twenty feet on to the next branch.

"You see, what I *meant* to do," he explained, as he turned head-over-heels, and crashed on to another branch thirty feet below, "what I *meant* to do—"

"Of course, it *was* rather—" he admitted, as he slithered very quickly through the next six branches.

"It all comes, I suppose," he decided, as he said good-bye to the last branch, spun round three times, and flew gracefully into a gorse-bush, "it all comes of *liking* honey so much. Oh, help!"

He crawled out of the gorse-bush, brushed the prickles from his nose, and began to think again. And the first person he thought of was Christopher Robin.

("*Was that me?*" *said Christopher Robin in an awed voice,*
hardly daring to believe it.

"*That was you.*"

Christopher Robin said nothing, but his eyes got larger and
larger, and his face got pinker and pinker.)

So Winnie-the-Pooh went round to his friend Christopher Robin, who lived behind a green door in another part of the forest.

"Good morning, Christopher Robin," he said.

"Good morning, Winnie-*ther*-Pooh," said you.

"I wonder if you've got such a thing as a balloon about you?"

"A balloon?"

"Yes, I just said to myself coming along: 'I wonder if Christopher Robin has such a thing as a balloon about him?' I just said it to myself, thinking of balloons, and wondering."

"What do you want a balloon for?" you said.

Winnie-the-Pooh looked round to see that nobody was listening, put his paw to his mouth, and said in a deep whisper: "*Honey!*"

"But you don't get honey with balloons!"

"*I* do," said Pooh.

Well, it just happened that you had been to a party the day before at the house of your friend Piglet, and you had balloons at the party. You had had a big green balloon; and one of Rabbit's relations had had a big blue one, and had left it behind, being really too young to go to a party at all; and so you had brought the green one *and* the blue one home with you.

"Which one would you like?" you asked Pooh.

He put his head between his paws and thought very carefully.

"It's like this," he said. "When you go after honey with a balloon, the great thing is not to let the bees know you're coming. Now, if you have a green balloon, they might think you were only part of the tree, and not notice you, and if you have a blue balloon, they might think you were only part of the sky, and not notice you, and the question is: Which is most likely?"

"Wouldn't they notice *you* underneath the balloon?" you asked.

"They might or they might not," said Winnie-the-Pooh. "You never can tell with bees." He thought for a moment and said: "I shall try to look like a small black cloud. That will deceive them."

"Then you had better have the blue balloon," you said; and so it was decided.

Well, you both went out with the blue balloon, and you took your gun with you, just in case, as you always did, and Winnie-the-Pooh went to a very muddy place that he knew of, and rolled and rolled until he was black all over; and

then, when the balloon was blown up as big as big, and you and Pooh were both holding on to the string, you let go suddenly, and Pooh Bear floated gracefully up into the sky, and stayed there—level with the top of the tree and about twenty feet away from it.

"Hooray!" you shouted.

"Isn't that fine?" shouted Winnie-the-Pooh down to you. "What do I look like?"

"You look like a Bear holding on to a balloon," you said.

"Not," said Pooh anxiously, "—not like a small black cloud in a blue sky?"

"Not very much."

"Ah, well, perhaps from up here it looks different. And, as I say, you never can tell with bees."

There was no wind to blow him nearer to the tree, so there he stayed. He could see the honey, he could smell the honey, but he couldn't quite reach the honey.

After a little while he called down to you.

"Christopher Robin!" he said in a loud whisper.

"Hallo!"

"I think the bees *suspect* something!"

"What sort of thing?"

"I don't know. But something tells me that they're *suspicious*!"

"Perhaps they think that you're after their honey."

"It may be that. You never can tell with bees."

There was another little silence, and then he called down to you again.

"Christopher Robin!"

"Yes?"

"Have you an umbrella in your house?"

"I think so."

"I wish you would bring it out here, and walk up and down with it, and look up at me every now and then, and say 'Tut-tut, it looks like rain.' I think, if you did that, it would help the deception which we are practising on these bees."

Well, you laughed to yourself, "Silly old Bear!" but you didn't say it aloud because you were so fond of him, and you went home for your umbrella.

"Oh, there you are!" called down Winnie-the-Pooh, as soon as you got back to the tree. "I was beginning to get anxious. I have discovered that the bees are now definitely Suspicious."

"Shall I put my umbrella up?" you said.

"Yes, but wait a moment. We must be practical. The important bee to deceive is the Queen Bee. Can you see which is the Queen Bee from down there?"

"No."

"A pity. Well, now, if you walk up and down with your

umbrella, saying, 'Tut-tut, it looks like rain,' I shall do what I can by singing a little Cloud Song, such as a cloud might sing. . . . Go!"

So, while you walked up and down and wondered if it would rain, Winnie-the-Pooh sang this song:

> How sweet to be a Cloud
>   Floating in the Blue!
> Every little cloud
> *Always* sings aloud.

> "How sweet to be a Cloud
>   Floating in the Blue!"
> It makes him very proud
> To be a little cloud.

The bees were still buzzing as suspiciously as ever. Some of them, indeed, left their nest and flew all round the cloud as it began the second verse of this song, and one bee sat down on the nose of the cloud for a moment, and then got up again.

"Christopher—*ow!*—Robin," called out the cloud.

"Yes?"

"I have just been thinking, and I have come to a very important decision. *These are the wrong sort of bees.*"

"Are they?"

"Quite the wrong sort. So I should think they would make the wrong sort of honey, shouldn't you?"

"Would they?"

"Yes. So I think I shall come down."

"How?" asked you.

Winnie-the-Pooh hadn't thought about this. If he let go of the string, he would fall—*bump*—and he didn't like the idea of that. So he thought for a long time, and then he said:

"Christopher Robin, you must shoot the balloon with your gun. Have you got your gun?"

"Of course I have," you said. "But if I do that, it will spoil the balloon," you said.

"But if you *don't*," said Pooh, "I shall have to let go, and that would spoil *me*."

When you put it like this, you saw how it was, and you aimed very carefully at the balloon, and fired.

"*Ow!*" said Pooh.

"Did I miss?" you asked.

"You didn't exactly *miss*," said Pooh, "but you missed the *balloon*."

"I'm so sorry," you said, and you fired again, and this

time you hit the balloon, and the air came slowly out, and Winnie-the-Pooh floated down to the ground.

But his arms were so stiff from holding on to the string of the balloon all that time that they stayed up straight in the air for more than a week, and whenever a fly came and settled on his nose he had to blow it off. And I think—but I am not sure—that *that* is why he was always called Pooh.

"Is that the end of the story?" asked Christopher Robin.

"That's the end of that one. There are others."

"About Pooh and Me?"

"And Piglet and Rabbit and all of you. Don't you remember?"

"I do remember, and then when I try to remember, I forget."

"That day when Pooh and Piglet tried to catch the Heffalump—"

"They didn't catch it, did they?"

"No."

"Pooh couldn't, because he hasn't any brain. Did *I* catch it?"

"Well, that comes into the story."

Christopher Robin nodded.

"I do remember," he said, "only Pooh doesn't very well,

so that's why he likes having it told to him again. Because then it's a real story and not just a remembering."

"That's just how *I* feel," I said.

Christopher Robin gave a deep sigh, picked his Bear up by the leg, and walked off to the door, trailing Pooh behind him. At the door he turned and said, "Coming to see me have my bath?"

"I might," I said.

"I didn't hurt him when I shot him, did I?"

"Not a bit."

He nodded and went out, and in a moment I heard Winnie-the-Pooh—*bump, bump, bump*—going up the stairs behind him.

CHAPTER II

In Which
Pooh Goes Visiting
and Gets Into a Tight Place

Edward Bear, known to his friends as Winnie-the-Pooh, or Pooh for short, was walking through the forest one day, humming proudly to himself. He had

made up a little hum that very morning, as he was doing his Stoutness Exercises in front of the glass: *Tra-la-la, tra-la-la*, as he stretched up as high as he could go, and then *Tra-la-la, tra-la—oh, help!—la*, as he tried to reach his toes. After breakfast he had said it over and over to himself until he had learnt it off by heart, and now he was humming it right through, properly. It went like this:

Tra-la-la, tra-la-la,
Tra-la-la, tra-la-la,
Rum-tum-tiddle-um-tum.
Tiddle-iddle, tiddle-iddle,
Tiddle-iddle, tiddle-iddle,
Rum-tum-tum-tiddle-um.

Well, he was humming this hum to himself, and walking along gaily, wondering what everybody else was doing, and what it felt like, being somebody else, when suddenly he came to a sandy bank, and in the bank was a large hole.

"Aha!" said Pooh. (*Rum-tum-tiddle-um-tum.*) "If I know anything about anything, that hole means Rabbit," he said, "and Rabbit means Company," he said, "and Company means Food and Listening-to-Me-Humming and such like. *Rum-tum-tum-tiddle-um.*"

So he bent down, put his head into the hole, and called out:

"Is anybody at home?"

There was a sudden scuffling noise from inside the hole, and then silence.

"What I said was, 'Is anybody at home?'" called out Pooh very loudly.

"No!" said a voice; and then added, "You needn't shout so loud. I heard you quite well the first time."

"Bother!" said Pooh. "Isn't there anybody here at all?"

"Nobody."

Winnie-the-Pooh took his head out of the hole, and thought for a little, and he thought to himself, "There must be somebody there, because somebody must have *said* 'Nobody.'" So he put his head back in the hole, and said:

"Hallo, Rabbit, isn't that you?"

"No," said Rabbit, in a different sort of voice this time.

"But isn't that Rabbit's voice?"

"I don't *think* so," said Rabbit. "It isn't *meant* to be."

"Oh!" said Pooh.

He took his head out of the hole, and had another think, and then he put it back, and said:

"Well, could you very kindly tell me where Rabbit is?"

"He has gone to see his friend Pooh Bear, who is a great friend of his."

"But this *is* Me!" said Bear, very much surprised.

"What sort of Me?"

"Pooh Bear."

"Are you sure?" said Rabbit, still more surprised.

"Quite, quite sure," said Pooh.

"Oh, well, then, come in."

So Pooh pushed and pushed and pushed his way through the hole, and at last he got in.

"You were quite right," said Rabbit, looking at him all over. "It *is* you. Glad to see you."

"Who did you think it was?"

"Well, I wasn't sure. You know how it is in the Forest. One can't have *anybody* coming into one's house. One has to be *careful*. What about a mouthful of something?"

Pooh always liked a little something at eleven o'clock in the morning, and he was very glad to see Rabbit getting out the plates and mugs; and when Rabbit said, "Honey or condensed milk with your bread?" he was so excited that he said, "Both," and then, so as not to seem greedy, he added, "But don't bother about the bread, please." And for a long time after that he said nothing . . . until at last, humming to himself in a rather sticky voice, he got up, shook Rabbit lovingly by the paw, and said that he must be going on.

"Must you?" said Rabbit politely.

"Well," said Pooh, "I could stay a little longer if it—if you—" and he tried very hard to look in the direction of the larder.

"As a matter of fact," said Rabbit, "I was going out myself directly."

"Oh, well, then, I'll be going on. Good-bye."

"Well, good-bye, if you're sure you won't have any more."

"*Is* there any more?" asked Pooh quickly.

Rabbit took the covers off the dishes, and said, "No, there wasn't."

"I thought not," said Pooh, nodding to himself. "Well, good-bye. I must be going on."

So he started to climb out of the hole. He pulled with his front paws, and pushed with his back paws, and in a little while his nose was out in the open again . . . and then his ears . . . and then his front paws . . . and then his shoulders . . . and then—

"Oh, help!" said Pooh. "I'd better go back."

"Oh, bother!" said Pooh. "I shall have to go on."

"I can't do either!" said Pooh. "Oh, help *and* bother!"

Now by this time Rabbit wanted to go for a walk too, and finding the front door full, he went out by the back door, and came round to Pooh, and looked at him.

"Hallo, are you stuck?" he asked.

"N-no," said Pooh carelessly. "Just resting and thinking and humming to myself."

"Here, give us a paw."

Pooh Bear stretched out a paw, and Rabbit pulled and pulled and pulled. . . .

"*Ow!*" cried Pooh. "You're hurting!"

"The fact is," said Rabbit, "you're stuck."

"It all comes," said Pooh crossly, "of not having front doors big enough."

"It all comes," said Rabbit sternly, "of eating too much. I thought at the time," said Rabbit, "only I didn't like to say anything," said Rabbit, "that one of us was eating too much," said Rabbit, "and I knew it wasn't *me*," he said. "Well, well, I shall go and fetch Christopher Robin."

Christopher Robin lived at the other end of the Forest, and when he came back with Rabbit, and saw the front half of Pooh, he said, "Silly old Bear," in such a loving voice that everybody felt quite hopeful again.

"I was just beginning to think," said Bear, sniffing slightly, "that Rabbit might never be able to use his front door again. And I should *hate* that," he said.

"So should I," said Rabbit.

"Use his front door again?" said Christopher Robin. "Of course he'll use his front door again."

"Good," said Rabbit.

"If we can't pull you out, Pooh, we might push you back."

Rabbit scratched his whiskers thoughtfully, and pointed out that, when once Pooh was pushed back, he was back, and of course nobody was more glad to see Pooh than *he* was, still there it was, some lived in trees and some lived underground, and—

"You mean I'd *never* get out?" said Pooh.

"I mean," said Rabbit, "that having got *so* far, it seems a pity to waste it."

Christopher Robin nodded.

"Then there's only one thing to be done," he said. "We shall have to wait for you to get thin again."

"How long does getting thin take?" asked Pooh anxiously.

"About a week, I should think."

"But I can't stay here for a *week*!"

"You can *stay* here all right, silly old Bear. It's getting you out which is so difficult."

"We'll read to you," said Rabbit cheerfully. "And I hope it won't snow," he added. "And I say, old fellow, you're taking up a good deal of room in my house—*do* you mind if I use your back legs as a towel-horse? Because, I mean, there they are—doing nothing—and it would be very convenient just to hang the towels on them."

"A week!" said Pooh gloomily. "*What about meals?*"

"I'm afraid no meals," said Christopher Robin, "because of getting thin quicker. But we *will* read to you."

Bear began to sigh, and then found he couldn't because he was so tightly stuck; and a tear rolled down his eye, as he said:

"Then would you read a Sustaining Book, such as would help and comfort a Wedged Bear in Great Tightness?"

So for a week Christopher Robin read that sort of book at the North end of Pooh,

and Rabbit

hung his washing on the South end . . . and in between Bear felt himself getting slenderer and slenderer. And at the end of the week Christopher Robin said, "*Now!*"

So he took hold of Pooh's front paws and Rabbit took hold of Christopher Robin, and all Rabbit's friends and relations took hold of Rabbit, and they all pulled together. . . .

And for a long time Pooh only said "*Ow!*" . . .

And "*Oh!*" . . .

And then, all of a sudden, he said "*Pop!*" just as if a cork were coming out of a bottle.

And Christopher Robin
and Rabbit and all Rabbit's
friends and relations went
head-over-heels backwards . . .
and on the top of them came
Winnie-the-Pooh—free!

So, with a nod of thanks to
his friends, he went on with his
walk through the forest, humming proudly to himself. But,
Christopher Robin looked
after him lovingly, and said to
himself, "Silly old Bear!"

CHAPTER III

In Which
Pooh and Piglet Go Hunting
and Nearly Catch a Woozle

The Piglet lived in a very grand house in the middle of a beech-tree, and the beech-tree was in the middle of the forest, and the Piglet lived in the middle of the house. Next to his house was a piece of broken board which had: "TRESPASSERS W" on it. When Christopher Robin asked the Piglet what it meant, he said it was his grandfather's name, and had been in the family for a long time, Christopher Robin said you *couldn't* be called Trespassers W, and Piglet said yes, you could, because his grandfather was, and it was short for Trespassers Will, which was short for Trespassers William. And his grandfather had had two names in case he lost one—Trespassers after an uncle, and William after Trespassers.

"I've got two names," said Christopher Robin carelessly.

"Well, there you are, that proves it," said Piglet.

One fine winter's day when Piglet was brushing away the snow in front of his house, he happened to look up, and there was Winnie-the-Pooh. Pooh was walking round and round in a circle, thinking of something else, and when Piglet called to him, he just went on walking.

"Hallo!" said Piglet, "what are *you* doing?"

"Hunting," said Pooh.

"Hunting what?"

"Tracking something," said Winnie-the-Pooh very mysteriously.

"Tracking what?" said Piglet, coming closer.

"That's just what I ask myself. I ask myself, What?"

"What do you think you'll answer?"

"I shall have to wait until I catch up with it," said Winnie-the-Pooh. "Now, look there." He pointed to the ground in front of him. "What do you see there?"

"Tracks," said Piglet. "Paw-marks." He gave a little squeak of excitement. "Oh, Pooh! Do think it's a—a—a Woozle?"

"It may be," said Pooh. "Sometimes it is, and sometimes it isn't. You never can tell with paw-marks."

With these few words he went on tracking, and Piglet, after watching him for a minute or two, ran after him. Winnie-the-Pooh had come to a sudden stop, and was bending over the tracks in a puzzled sort of way.

"What's the matter?" asked Piglet.

"It's a very funny thing," said Bear, "but there seem to be *two* animals now. This—whatever-it-was—has been joined by another—whatever-it-is—and the two of them are now proceeding in company. Would you mind coming with me, Piglet, in case they turn out to be Hostile Animals?"

Piglet scratched his ear in a nice sort of way, and said that he had nothing to do until Friday, and would be delighted to come, in case it really *was* a Woozle.

"You mean, in case it really is two Woozles," said Winnie-the-Pooh, and Piglet said that anyhow he had nothing to do until Friday. So off they went together.

There was a small spinney of larch trees just here, and it seemed as if the two Woozles, if that is what they were, had been going round this spinney; so round this spinney went Pooh and Piglet after them; Piglet passing the time by telling Pooh what his Grandfather Trespassers W had done to Remove Stiffness after Tracking, and how his Grandfather Trespassers W had suffered in his later years from Shortness of Breath, and other matters of interest, and Pooh wondering what a Grandfather was like, and if perhaps this was

Two Grandfathers they were after now, and, if so, whether he would be allowed to take one home and keep it, and what Christopher Robin would say. And still the tracks went on in front of them. . . .

Suddenly Winnie-the-Pooh stopped, and pointed excitedly in front of him. "*Look!*"

"*What?*" said Piglet, with a jump. And then, to show that he hadn't been frightened, he jumped up and down once or twice in an exercising sort of way.

"The tracks!" said Pooh. "*A third animal has joined the other two!*"

"Pooh!" cried Piglet. "Do you think it is another Woozle?"

"No," said Pooh, "because it makes different marks. It is

either Two Woozles and one, as it might be, Wizzle, or Two, as it might be, Wizzles and one, if so it is, Woozle. Let us continue to follow them."

So they went on, feeling just a little anxious now, in case the three animals in front of them were of Hostile Intent. And Piglet wished very much that his Grandfather T. W. were there, instead of elsewhere, and Pooh thought how nice it would be if they met Christopher Robin suddenly but quite accidentally, and only because he liked Christopher Robin so much. And then, all of a sudden, Winnie-the-Pooh stopped again, and licked the tip of his

nose in a cooling manner, for he was feeling more hot and anxious than ever in his life before. *There were four animals in front of them!*

"Do you see, Piglet? Look at their tracks! Three, as it were, Woozles, and one, as it was, Wizzle. *Another Woozle has joined them!*"

And so it seemed to be. There were the tracks; crossing over each other here, getting muddled up with each other there; but, quite plainly every now and then, the tracks of four sets of paws.

"I *think*," said Piglet, when he had licked the tip of his nose too, and found that it brought very little comfort, "I *think* that I have just remembered something. I have just remembered something that I forgot to do yesterday and shan't be able to do tomorrow. So I suppose I really ought to go back and do it now."

"We'll do it this afternoon, and I'll come with you," said Pooh.

"It isn't the sort of thing you can do in the afternoon," said Piglet quickly. "It's a very particular morning thing, that has to be done in the morning, and, if possible, between the hours of— What would you say the time was?"

"About twelve," said Winnie-the-Pooh, looking at the sun.

"Between, as I was saying, the hours of twelve and twelve five. So, really, dear old Pooh, if you'll excuse me— *What's that?*"

Pooh looked up at the sky, and then, as he heard the

whistle again, he looked up into the branches of a big oak-tree, and then he saw a friend of his.

"It's Christopher Robin," he said.

"Ah, then you'll be all right," said Piglet. "You'll be quite safe with *him*. Good-bye," and he trotted off home as quickly as he could, very glad to be Out of All Danger again.

Christopher Robin came slowly down his tree.

"Silly old Bear," he said, "what *were* you doing? First you went round the spinney twice by yourself, and then Piglet ran after you and you went round again together, and then you were just going round a fourth time—"

"Wait a moment," said Winnie-the-Pooh, holding up his paw.

He sat down and thought, in the most thoughtful way he could think. Then he fitted his paw into one of the Tracks . . . and then he scratched his nose twice, and stood up.

"Yes," said Winnie-the-Pooh.

"I see now," said Winnie-the-Pooh.

"I have been Foolish and Deluded," said he, "and I am a Bear of No Brain at All."

"You're the Best Bear in All the World," said Christopher Robin soothingly.

"Am I?" said Pooh hopefully. And then he brightened up suddenly.

"Anyhow," he said, "it is nearly Luncheon Time."

So he went home for it.

CHAPTER IV

In Which

Eeyore Loses a Tail and Pooh Finds One

The Old Grey Donkey, Eeyore, stood by himself in a thistly corner of the forest, his front feet well apart, his head on one side, and thought about things. Sometimes he thought sadly to himself, "Why?" and sometimes he

thought, "Wherefore?" and sometimes he thought, "Inasmuch as which?"—and sometimes he didn't quite know what he *was* thinking about. So when Winnie-the-Pooh came stumping along, Eeyore was very glad to be able to stop thinking for a little, in order to say "How do you do?" in a gloomy manner to him.

"And how are you?" said Winnie-the-Pooh.

Eeyore shook his head from side to side.

"Not very how," he said. "I don't seem to have felt at all how for a long time."

"Dear, dear," said Pooh, "I'm sorry about that. Let's have a look at you."

So Eeyore stood there, gazing sadly at the ground, and Winnie-the-Pooh walked all round him once.

"Why, what's happened to your tail?" he said in surprise.

"What *has* happened to it?" said Eeyore.

"It isn't there!"

"Are you sure?"

"Well, either a tail *is* there or it isn't there. You can't make a mistake about it. And yours *isn't* there!"

"Then what is?"

"Nothing."

"Let's have a look," said Eeyore, and he turned slowly round to the place where his tail had been a little while ago, and then, finding that he couldn't catch it up, he turned round the other way, until he came back to where he was at first, and then he put his head down and looked between his front legs, and at last he said, with a long, sad sigh, "I believe you're right."

"Of course I'm right," said Pooh.

"That Accounts for a Good Deal," said Eeyore gloomily. "It Explains Everything. No Wonder."

"You must have left it somewhere," said Winnie-the-Pooh.

"Somebody must have taken it," said Eeyore. "How Like Them," he added, after a long silence.

Pooh felt that he ought to say something helpful about it, but didn't quite know what. So he decided to do something helpful instead.

"Eeyore," he said solemnly, "I, Winnie-the-Pooh, will find your tail for you."

"Thank you, Pooh," answered Eeyore. "You're a real friend," said he. "Not like Some," he said.

So Winnie-the-Pooh went off to find Eeyore's tail.

It was a fine spring morning in the forest as he started out. Little soft clouds played happily in a blue sky, skipping from time to time in front of the sun as if they had come to put it out, and then sliding away suddenly so that the next might have his turn. Through them and between them the sun shone bravely; and a copse which had worn its firs all the year round seemed old and dowdy now beside the new green lace which the beeches had put on so prettily. Through copse and spinney marched Bear; down open slopes of gorse and heather, over rocky beds of streams, up steep banks of sandstone into the heather again; and so at last, tired and hungry, to the Hundred Acre Wood. For it was in the Hundred Acre Wood that Owl lived.

"And if anyone knows anything about anything," said Bear to himself, "it's Owl who knows something about something," he said, "or my name's not Winnie-the-Pooh," he said. "Which it is," he added. "So there you are."

Owl lived at The Chestnuts, an old-world residence of great charm, which was grander than anybody else's, or seemed so to Bear, because it had both a knocker *and* a bell-pull. Underneath the knocker there was a notice which said:

PLES RING IF AN RNSER IS REQIRD.

Underneath the bell-pull there was a notice which said:

PLEZ CNOKE IF AN RNSR IS NOT REQID.

These notices had been written by Christopher Robin, who was the only one in the forest who could spell; for Owl, wise though he was in many ways, able to read and write and spell his own name WOL, yet somehow went all to pieces over delicate words like MEASLES and BUTTERED TOAST.

Winnie-the-Pooh read the two notices very carefully, first from left to right, and afterwards, in case he had missed some of it, from right to left. Then, to make quite sure, he knocked and pulled the knocker, and he pulled and knocked the bell-rope, and he called out in a very loud voice, "Owl! I require an answer! It's Bear speaking." And the door opened, and Owl looked out.

"Hallo, Pooh," he said. "How's things?"

"Terrible and Sad," said Pooh, "because Eeyore, who is a friend of mine, has lost his tail. And he's Moping about it. So could you very kindly tell me how to find it for him?"

"Well," said Owl, "the customary procedure in such cases is as follows."

"What does Crustimoney Proseedcake mean?" said Pooh. "For I am a Bear of Very Little Brain, and long words Bother me."

"It means the Thing to Do."

"As long as it means that, I don't mind," said Pooh humbly.

"The thing to do is as follows. First, Issue a Reward. Then—"

"Just a moment," said Pooh, holding up his paw. "*What* do we do to this—what you were saying? You sneezed just as you were going to tell me."

"I *didn't* sneeze."

"Yes, you did, Owl."

"Excuse me, Pooh, I didn't. You can't sneeze without knowing it."

"Well, you can't know it without something having been sneezed."

"What I *said* was, 'First *Issue* a Reward.'"

"You're doing it again," said Pooh sadly.

"A Reward!" said Owl very loudly. "We write a notice to say that we will give a large something to anybody who finds Eeyore's tail."

"I see, I see," said Pooh, nodding his head. "Talking about large somethings," he went on dreamily, "I generally have a small something about now—about this time in the morning," and he looked wistfully at the cupboard in the corner of Owl's parlour; "just a mouthful of condensed milk or what not, with perhaps a lick of honey—"

"Well, then," said Owl, "we write out this notice, and we put it up all over the forest."

"A lick of honey," murmured Bear to himself, "or—or not, as the case may be." And he gave a deep sigh, and tried very hard to listen to what Owl was saying.

But Owl went on and on, using longer and longer words, until at last he came back to where he started, and he explained that the person to write out this notice was Christopher Robin.

"It was he who wrote the ones on my front door for me. Did you see them, Pooh?"

For some time now Pooh had been saying "Yes" and "No" in turn, with his eyes shut, to all that Owl was saying, and having said, "Yes, yes," last time, he said "No, not at all," now, without really knowing what Owl was talking about.

"Didn't you see them?" said Owl, a little surprised. "Come and look at them now."

So they went outside. And Pooh looked at the knocker and the notice below it, and he looked at the bell-rope and the notice below it, and the more he looked at the bell-rope, the more he felt that he had seen something like it, somewhere else, sometime before.

"Handsome bell-rope, isn't it?" said Owl.

Pooh nodded.

"It reminds me of something," he said, "but I can't think what. Where did you get it?"

"I just came across it in the Forest. It was hanging over a
bush, and I thought at first somebody lived there, so I rang
it, and nothing happened, and then I rang it again very
loudly, and it came off in my hand, and as nobody seemed
to want it, I took it home, and—"

"Owl," said Pooh solemnly, "you made a mistake. Somebody did want it."

"Who?"

"Eeyore. My dear friend Eeyore. He was—he was fond of it."

"Fond of it?"

"Attached to it," said Winnie-the-Pooh sadly.

So with these words he unhooked it, and carried it back to Eeyore; and when Christopher Robin had nailed

it on in its right place again, Eeyore frisked about the forest, waving his tail so happily that Winnie-the-Pooh came over all funny, and had to hurry home for a little snack of something to sustain him. And, wiping his mouth half an hour afterwards, he sang to himself proudly:

Who found the Tail?
   "I," said Pooh,
"At a quarter to two
   (Only it was quarter to eleven really),
I found the Tail!"

CHAPTER V

In Which
Piglet Meets a Heffalump

One day, when Christopher Robin and Winnie-the-Pooh and Piglet were all talking together, Christopher Robin finished the mouthful he was eating and said carelessly: "I saw a Heffalump to-day, Piglet."

"What was it doing?" asked Piglet.

"Just lumping along," said Christopher Robin. "I don't think it saw *me*."

"I saw one once," said Piglet. "At least, I think I did," he said. "Only perhaps it wasn't."

"So did I," said Pooh, wondering what a Heffalump was like.

"You don't often see them," said Christopher Robin carelessly.

"Not now," said Piglet.

"Not at this time of year," said Pooh.

Then they all talked about something else, until it was

time for Pooh and Piglet to go home together. At first as
they stumped along the path which edged the Hundred
Acre Wood, they didn't say much to each other; but when
they came to the stream and had helped each other across
the stepping stones, and were able to walk side by side
again over the heather, they began to talk in a friendly way
about this and that, and Piglet said, "If you see what I mean,
Pooh," and Pooh said, "It's just what I think myself, Piglet,"
and Piglet said, "But, on the other hand, Pooh, we must
remember," and Pooh said, "Quite true, Piglet, although
I had forgotten it for the moment." And then, just as they
came to the Six Pine Trees, Pooh looked round to see that
nobody else was listening, and said in a very solemn voice:

"Piglet, I have decided something."

"What have you decided, Pooh?"

"I have decided to catch a Heffalump."

Pooh nodded his head several times as he said this, and waited for Piglet to say "How?" or "Pooh, you couldn't!" or something helpful of that sort, but Piglet said nothing. The fact was Piglet was wishing that *he* had thought about it first.

"I shall do it," said Pooh, after waiting a little longer, "by means of a trap. And it must be a Cunning Trap, so you will have to help me, Piglet."

"Pooh," said Piglet, feeling quite happy again now, "I will." And then he said, "How shall we do it?" and Pooh said, "That's just it. How?" And then they sat down together to think it out.

Pooh's first idea was that they should dig a Very Deep Pit, and then the Heffalump would come along and fall into the Pit, and—

"Why?" said Piglet.

"Why what?" said Pooh.

"Why would he fall in?"

Pooh rubbed his nose with his paw, and said that the Heffalump might be walking along, humming a little song, and looking up at the sky, wondering if it would rain, and so he wouldn't see the Very Deep Pit until he was half-way down, when it would be too late.

Piglet said that this was a very good Trap, but supposing it were raining already?

Pooh rubbed his nose again, and said that he hadn't thought of that. And then he brightened up, and said that, if it were raining already, the Heffalump would be looking at the sky wondering if it would *clear up*, and so he wouldn't see the Very Deep Pit until he was half-way down. . . . When it would be too late.

Piglet said that, now that this point had been explained, he thought it was a Cunning Trap.

Pooh was very proud when he heard this, and he felt that the Heffalump was as good as caught already, but there was just one other thing which had to be thought about, and it was this. *Where should they dig the Very Deep Pit?*

Piglet said that the best place would be somewhere where a Heffalump was, just before he fell into it, only about a foot farther on.

"But then he would see us digging it," said Pooh.

"Not if he was looking at the sky."

"He would Suspect," said Pooh, "if he happened to look down." He thought for a long time and then added sadly, "It isn't as easy as I thought. I suppose that's why Heffalumps hardly *ever* get caught."

"That must be it," said Piglet.

They sighed and got up; and when they had taken a few gorse prickles out of themselves they sat down again; and all the time Pooh was saying to himself, "If only I could *think* of something!" For he felt sure that a Very Clever Brain could catch a Heffalump if only he knew the right way to go about it.

"Suppose," he said to Piglet, "*you* wanted to catch *me*, how would you do it?"

"Well," said Piglet, "I should do it like this. I should make a Trap, and I should put a Jar of Honey in the Trap, and you would smell it, and you would go in after it, and—"

"And I would go in after it," said Pooh excitedly, "only very carefully so as not to hurt myself, and I would get to the Jar of Honey, and I should lick round the edges first of all, pretending that there wasn't any more, you know, and then I should walk away and think about it a little, and then I should come back and start licking in the middle of the jar, and then—"

"Yes, well never mind about that. There you would be, and there I should catch you. Now the first thing to think of is, What do Heffalumps like? I should think acorns, shouldn't you? We'll get a lot of— I say, wake up, Pooh!"

Pooh, who had gone into a happy dream, woke up with a start, and said that Honey was a much more trappy thing than Haycorns. Piglet didn't think so; and they were just going to argue about it, when Piglet remembered that, if they put acorns in the Trap, *he* would have to find the acorns, but if they put honey, then Pooh would have to give up some of his own honey, so he said, "All right, honey then," just as Pooh remembered it too, and was going to say, "All right, haycorns."

"Honey," said Piglet to himself in a thoughtful way, as if it were now settled. "*I'll* dig the pit, while *you* go and get the honey."

"Very well," said Pooh, and he stumped off.

As soon as he got home, he went to the larder; and he stood on a chair, and took down a very large jar of honey from the top shelf. It had HUNNY written on it, but, just to make sure, he took off the paper cover and looked at it, and it *looked* just like honey. "But you never can tell," said Pooh. "I remember my uncle saying once that he had seen cheese just this colour." So he put his tongue in, and took a large lick. "Yes," he said, "it is. No doubt about that. And honey, I should

say, right down to the bottom of the jar. Unless, of course," he said, "somebody put cheese in at the bottom just for a joke. Perhaps I had better go a *little* further . . . just in case . . . in case Heffalumps *don't* like cheese . . . same as me. . . . Ah!" And he gave a deep sigh. "I *was* right. It *is* honey, right the way down."

Having made certain of this, he took the jar back to

Piglet, and Piglet looked up from the bottom of his Very Deep Pit, and said, "Got it?" and Pooh said, "Yes, but it isn't quite a full jar," and he threw it down to Piglet, and Piglet said, "No, it isn't! Is that all you've got left?" and Pooh said "Yes." Because it was. So Piglet put the jar at the bottom of the Pit, and climbed out, and they went off home together.

"Well, good night, Pooh," said Piglet, when they had got to Pooh's house. "And we meet at six o'clock tomorrow morning by the Pine Trees, and see how many Heffalumps we've got in our Trap."

"Six o'clock, Piglet. And have you got any string?"

"No. Why do you want string?"

"To lead them home with."

"Oh! . . . I *think* Heffalumps come if you whistle."

"Some do and some don't. You never can tell with Heffalumps. Well, good night!"

"Good night!"

And off Piglet trotted to his house TRESPASSERS W, while Pooh made his preparations for bed.

Some hours later, just as the night was beginning to steal away, Pooh woke up suddenly with a sinking feeling. He had had that sinking feeling before, and he knew what it meant. *He was hungry.* So he went to the larder, and he stood on a chair and reached up to the top shelf, and found—nothing.

"That's funny," he thought. "I know I had a jar of honey there. A full jar, full of honey right up to the top, and it had HUNNY written on it, so that I should know it was honey.

That's very funny." And then he began to wander up and down, wondering where it was and murmuring a murmur to himself. Like this:

> It's very, very funny,
> 'Cos I *know* I had some honey;
> 'Cos it had a label on,
>   Saying HUNNY.

> A goloptious full-up pot too,
> And I don't know where it's got to,
> No, I don't know where it's gone—
>   Well, it's funny.

He had murmured this to himself three times in a singing sort of way, when suddenly he remembered. He had put it into the Cunning Trap to catch the Heffalump.

"Bother!" said Pooh. "It all comes of trying to be kind to Heffalumps." And he got back into bed.

But he couldn't sleep. The more he tried to sleep, the more he couldn't. He tried Counting Sheep, which is sometimes a good way of getting to sleep, and, as that was no good, he tried counting Heffalumps. And that was worse. Because every Heffalump that he counted was making straight for a pot of Pooh's honey, *and eating it all*. For some minutes he lay there miserably, but when the five hundred and eighty-seventh Heffalump was licking its jaws, and saying to itself,

"Very good honey this, I don't know when I've tasted better," Pooh could bear it no longer. He jumped out of bed, he ran out of the house, and he ran straight to the Six Pine Trees.

The Sun was still in bed, but there was a lightness in the sky over the Hundred Acre Wood which seemed to show that it was waking up and would soon be kicking off the clothes. In the half-light the Pine Trees looked cold and lonely, and the Very Deep Pit seemed deeper than it was, and Pooh's jar of honey at the bottom was something

mysterious, a shape and no more. But as he got nearer to it his nose told him that it was indeed honey, and his tongue came out and began to polish up his mouth, ready for it.

"Bother!" said Pooh, as he got his nose inside the jar. "A Heffalump has been eating it!" And then he thought a little and said, "Oh, no, *I* did. I forgot."

Indeed, he had eaten most of it. But there was a little left at the very bottom of the jar, and he pushed his head right in, and began to lick. . . .

By and by Piglet woke up. As soon as he woke he said to himself, "Oh!" Then he said bravely, "Yes," and then, still more bravely, "Quite so." But he didn't feel very brave, for the word which was really jiggeting about in his brain was "Heffalumps."

What was a Heffalump like?

Was it Fierce?

Did it come when you whistled? And *how* did it come?

Was it Fond of Pigs at all?

If it was Fond of Pigs, did it make any difference *what sort of Pig*?

Supposing it was Fierce with Pigs, would it make any difference *if the Pig had a grandfather called* TRESPASSERS WILLIAM?

He didn't know the answer to any of these questions . . . and he was going to see his first Heffalump in about an hour from now!

 Of course Pooh would be with him, and it was much more Friendly with two. But suppose Heffalumps were Very Fierce with Pigs *and* Bears? Wouldn't it be better to pretend that he had a headache, and couldn't go up to the Six Pine Trees this morning? But then suppose that it was a very fine day, and there was no Heffalump in the trap, here he would be, in bed all the morning, simply wasting his time for nothing. What should he do?

And then he had a Clever Idea. He would go up very quietly to the Six Pine Trees now, peep very cautiously into the Trap, and see if there *was* a Heffalump there. And if there was, he would go back to bed, and if there wasn't, he wouldn't.

So off he went. At first he thought that there wouldn't be a Heffalump in the Trap, and then he thought that there would, and as he got nearer he

was *sure* that there would, because he could hear it heffalumping about it like anything.

"Oh, dear, oh, dear, oh, dear!" said Piglet to himself. And he wanted to run away. But somehow, having got so near, he felt that he must just see what a Heffalump was like. So he crept to the side of the Trap and looked in. . . .

And all the time Winnie-the-Pooh had been trying to get the honey-jar off his head. The more he shook it, the more tightly it stuck. "*Bother!*" he said, inside the jar, and "*Oh, help!*" and, mostly "*Ow!*" And he tried bumping it against things, but as he couldn't see what he was bumping it against, it didn't help him; and he tried to climb out of the Trap, but as he could see nothing but jar, and not much of that, he couldn't find his way. So at last he lifted up his head, jar and all, and made a loud, roaring noise of Sadness and Despair . . . and it was at that moment that Piglet looked down.

"Help, help!" cried Piglet, "a Heffalump, a Horrible Heffalump!" and he scampered off as hard as he could, still crying out, "Help, help, a Herrible Hoffalump! Hoff, Hoff, a Hellible Horralump! Holl, Holl, a Hoffable Hellerump!" And he didn't stop crying and scampering until he got to Christopher Robin's house.

"Whatever's the matter, Piglet?" said Christopher Robin, who was just getting up.

"Heff," said Piglet, breathing so hard that he could hardly speak, "a Hell—a Heff—a Heffalump."

"Where?"

"Up there," said Piglet, waving his paw.

"What did it look like?"

"Like—like— It had the biggest head you ever saw, Christopher Robin. A great enormous thing, like—like nothing. A huge big—well, like a—I don't know—like an enormous big nothing. Like a jar."

"Well," said Christopher Robin, putting on his shoes, "I shall go and look at it. Come on."

Piglet wasn't afraid if he had Christopher Robin with him, so off they went. . . .

"I can hear it, can't you?" said Piglet anxiously, as they got near.

"I can hear *something*," said Christopher Robin.

It was Pooh bumping his head against a tree-root he had found.

"There!" said Piglet. "Isn't it *awful*?" And he held on tight to Christopher Robin's hand.

Suddenly Christopher Robin began to laugh . . . and he laughed . . . and he laughed . . . and he laughed. And while he was still laughing—*Crash* went the Heffalump's head against the tree-root, Smash went the jar, and out came Pooh's head again. . . .

Then Piglet saw what a Foolish Piglet he had been, and he was so ashamed of himself that he ran straight off home and went to bed with a headache. But Christopher Robin and Pooh went home to breakfast together.

"Oh, Bear!" said Christopher Robin. "How I do love you!"

"So do I," said Pooh.

CHAPTER VI

In Which

Eeyore Has a Birthday and Gets Two Presents

Eeyore, the old grey Donkey, stood by the side of the stream, and looked at himself in the water.

"Pathetic," he said. "That's what it is. Pathetic."

He turned and walked slowly down the stream for twenty yards, splashed across it, and walked slowly back on the other side. Then he looked at himself in the water again.

"As I thought," he said. "No better from *this* side. But nobody minds. Nobody cares. Pathetic, that's what it is."

There was a crackling noise in the bracken behind him, and out came Pooh.

"Good morning, Eeyore," said Pooh.

"Good morning, Pooh Bear," said Eeyore gloomily. "If it *is* a good morning," he said. "Which I doubt," said he.

"Why, what's the matter?"

"Nothing, Pooh Bear, nothing. We can't all, and some of us don't. That's all there is to it."

"Can't all *what*?" said Pooh, rubbing his nose.

"Gaiety. Song-and-dance. Here we go round the mulberry bush."

"Oh!" said Pooh. He thought for a long time, and then asked, "What mulberry bush is that?"

"Bon-hommy," went on Eeyore gloomily. "French word meaning bonhommy," he explained. "I'm not complaining, but There It Is."

Pooh sat down on a large stone, and tried to think this out. It sounded to him like a riddle, and he was never much good at riddles, being a Bear of Very Little Brain. So he sang *Cottleston Pie* instead:

> Cottleston, Cottleston, Cottleston Pie,
> A fly can't bird, but a bird can fly.
> Ask me a riddle and I reply:
> "*Cottleston, Cottleston, Cottleston Pie.*"

That was the first verse. When he had finished it, Eeyore didn't actually say that he didn't like it, so Pooh very kindly sang the second verse to him:

> Cottleston, Cottleston, Cottleston Pie,
> A fish can't whistle and neither can I.
> Ask me a riddle and I reply:
> *"Cottleston, Cottleston, Cottleston Pie."*

Eeyore still said nothing at all, so Pooh hummed the third verse quietly to himself:

> Cottleston, Cottleston, Cottleston Pie,
> Why does a chicken, I don't know why.
> Ask me a riddle and I reply:
> *"Cottleston, Cottleston, Cottleston Pie."*

"That's right," said Eeyore. "Sing. Umty-tiddly, umty-too. Here we go gathering Nuts and May. Enjoy yourself."

"I am," said Pooh.
"Some can," said Eeyore.

81

"Why, what's the matter?"

"*Is* anything the matter?"

"You seem so sad, Eeyore."

"Sad? Why should I be sad? It's my birthday. The happiest day of the year."

"Your birthday?" said Pooh in great surprise.

"Of course it is. Can't you see? Look at all the presents I have had." He waved a foot from side to side. "Look at the birthday cake. Candles and pink sugar."

Pooh looked—first to the right and then to the left.

"Presents?" said Pooh. "Birthday cake?" said Pooh. "*Where?*"

"Can't you see them?"

"No," said Pooh.

"Neither can I," said Eeyore. "Joke," he explained. "Ha ha!"

Pooh scratched his head, being a little puzzled by all this.

"But is it really your birthday?" he asked.

"It is."

"Oh! Well, Many happy returns of the day, Eeyore."

"And many happy returns to you, Pooh Bear."

"But it isn't *my* birthday."

"No, it's mine."

"But you said 'Many happy returns—'"

"Well, why not? You don't always want to be miserable on my birthday, do you?"

"Oh, I see," said Pooh.

"It's bad enough," said Eeyore, almost breaking down, "being miserable myself, what with no presents and no cake and no candles, and no proper notice taken of me at all, but if everybody else is going to be miserable too—"

This was too much for Pooh. "Stay there!" he called to Eeyore, as he turned and hurried back home as quick as he could; for he felt that he must get poor Eeyore a present of *some* sort at once, and he could always think of a proper one afterwards.

Outside his house he found Piglet, jumping up and down trying to reach the knocker.

"Hallo, Piglet," he said.

"Hallo, Pooh," said Piglet.

"What are *you* trying to do?"

"I was trying to reach the knocker," said Piglet. "I just came round—"

"Let me do it for you," said Pooh kindly. So he reached up and knocked at the door. "I have just seen Eeyore," he began, "and poor Eeyore is in a Very Sad Condition, because it's his birthday, and nobody has taken any notice of it, and he's very Gloomy—you know what Eeyore is— and there he was, and— What a long time whoever lives here is answering this door." And he knocked again.

"But Pooh," said Piglet, "it's your own house!"

"Oh!" said Pooh. "So it is," he said. "Well, let's go in."

So in they went. The first thing Pooh did was to go to the cupboard to see if he had quite a small jar of honey left; and he had, so he took it down.

"I'm giving this to Eeyore," he explained, "as a present. What are *you* going to give?"

"Couldn't I give it too?" said Piglet. "From both of us?"

"No," said Pooh. "That would *not* be a good plan."

"All right, then, I'll give him a balloon. I've got one left from my party. I'll go and get it now, shall I?"

"That, Piglet, is a *very* good idea. It is just what Eeyore wants to cheer him up. Nobody can be uncheered with a balloon."

So off Piglet trotted; and in the other direction went Pooh, with his jar of honey.

It was a warm day, and he had a long way to go. He hadn't gone more than half-way when a sort of funny feeling began to creep all over him. It began at the tip of his nose and trickled all through him and out at the soles of his feet. It was just as if somebody inside him were saying,

"Now then, Pooh, time for a little something."

"Dear, dear," said Pooh, "I didn't know it was as late as that." So he sat down and took the top off his jar of honey. "Lucky I brought this with me," he thought. "Many a bear going out on a warm day like this would never have thought of bringing a little something with him." And he began to eat.

"Now let me see," he thought, as he took his last lick of the inside of the jar, "where was I going? Ah, yes, Eeyore." He got up slowly.

And then, suddenly, he remembered. He had eaten Eeyore's birthday present!

"*Bother!*" said Pooh. "What *shall* I do? I *must* give him *something.*"

For a little while he couldn't think of anything. Then he thought: "Well, it's a very nice pot, even if there's no honey in it, and if I washed it clean, and got somebody to write 'A Happy Birthday' on it, Eeyore could keep things in it, which might be Useful." So, as he was just passing the Hundred Acre Wood, he went inside to call on Owl, who lived there.

"Good morning, Owl," he said.

"Good morning, Pooh," said Owl.

"Many happy returns of Eeyore's birthday," said Pooh.

"Oh, is that what it is?"

"What are you giving him, Owl?"

"What are *you* giving him, Pooh?"

"I'm giving him a Useful Pot to Keep Things In, and I wanted to ask you—"

"Is this it?" said Owl, taking it out of Pooh's paw.

"Yes, and I wanted to ask you—"

"Somebody has been keeping honey in it," said Owl.

"You can keep *anything* in it," said Pooh earnestly. "It's Very Useful like that. And I wanted to ask you—"

"You ought to write 'A Happy Birthday' on it."

"*That* was what I wanted to ask you," said Pooh. "Because my spelling is Wobbly. It's good spelling but it Wobbles, and the letters get in the wrong places. Would *you* write 'A Happy Birthday' on it for me?"

"It's a nice pot," said Owl, looking at it all round. "Couldn't I give it too? From both of us?"

"No," said Pooh. "That would *not* be a good plan. Now I'll just wash it first, and then you can write on it."

Well, he washed the pot out, and dried it, while Owl licked the end of his pencil, and wondered how to spell "birthday."

"Can you read, Pooh?" he asked a little anxiously. "There's a notice about knocking and ringing outside my door, which Christopher Robin wrote. Could you read it?"

"Christopher Robin told me what it said, and *then* I could."

"Well, I'll tell you what *this* says, and then you'll be able to."

So Owl wrote . . . and this is what he wrote:

HIPY PAPY BTHUTHDTH THUTHDA

BTHUTHDY.

Pooh looked on admiringly.

"I'm just saying 'A Happy Birthday,'" said Owl carelessly.

"It's a nice long one," said Pooh, very much impressed by it.

"Well, *actually*, of course, I'm saying 'A Very Happy Birthday with love from Pooh.' Naturally it takes a good deal of pencil to say a long thing like that."

"Oh, I see," said Pooh.

While all this was happening, Piglet had gone back to his own house to get Eeyore's balloon. He held it very tightly against himself, so that it shouldn't blow away, and he ran as fast as he could so as to get to Eeyore before Pooh did; for he thought that he would like to be the first one to give a present, just as if he had thought of it without being told by anybody. And running along, and thinking how pleased Eeyore would be, he didn't look where he was going . . . and suddenly he put his foot in a rabbit hole, and fell down flat on his face.

BANG!!!???***!!!

Piglet lay there, wondering what had happened. At first he thought that the whole world had blown up; and then he thought that perhaps only the Forest part of it had; and then he thought that perhaps only *he* had, and he was now alone in the moon or somewhere, and would never see Christopher Robin or Pooh or Eeyore again. And then he thought, "Well, even if I'm in the moon, I needn't be face downwards all the time," so he got cautiously up and looked about him.

He was still in the Forest!

"Well, that's funny," he thought. "I wonder what that bang was. I couldn't have made such a noise just falling down. And where's my balloon? And what's that small piece of damp rag doing?"

It was the balloon!

"Oh, dear!" said Piglet. "Oh, dear, oh, dearie, dearie, dear! Well, it's too late now. I can't go back, and I haven't another balloon, and perhaps Eeyore doesn't *like* balloons so *very* much."

So he trotted on, rather sadly now, and down he came to the side of the stream where Eeyore was, and called out to him.

"Good morning, Eeyore," shouted Piglet.

"Good morning, Little Piglet," said Eeyore. "If it *is* a

good morning," he said. "Which I doubt," said he. "Not that it matters," he said.

"Many happy returns of the day," said Piglet, having now got closer.

Eeyore stopped looking at himself in the stream, and turned to stare at Piglet.

"Just say that again," he said.

"Many hap—"

"Wait a moment."

Balancing on three legs, he began to bring his fourth

leg very cautiously up to his ear. "I did this yesterday," he explained, as he fell down for the third time. "It's quite easy. It's so as I can hear better. . . . There, that's done it! Now then, what were you saying?" He pushed his ear forward with his hoof.

"Many happy returns of the day," said Piglet again.

"Meaning me?"

"Of course, Eeyore."

"My birthday?"

"Yes."

"Me having a real birthday?"

"Yes, Eeyore, and I've brought you a present."

Eeyore took down his right hoof from his right ear, turned round, and with great difficulty put up his left hoof.

"I must have that in the other ear," he said. "Now then."

"A present," said Piglet very loudly.

"Meaning me again?"

"Yes."

"My birthday still?"

"Of course, Eeyore."

"Me going on having a real birthday?"

"Yes, Eeyore, and I brought you a balloon."

"*Balloon?*" said Eeyore. "You did say balloon? One of those big coloured things you blow up? Gaiety, song-and-dance, here we are and there we are?"

"Yes, but I'm afraid—I'm very sorry, Eeyore—but when I was running along to bring it you, I fell down."

"Dear, dear, how unlucky! You ran too fast, I expect. You didn't hurt yourself, Little Piglet?"

"No, but I—I—oh, Eeyore, I burst the balloon!"

There was a very long silence.

"My balloon?" said Eeyore at last.

Piglet nodded.

"My birthday balloon?"

"Yes, Eeyore," said Piglet sniffing a little. "Here it is. With—with many happy returns of the day." And he gave Eeyore the small piece of damp rag.

"Is this it?" said Eeyore, a little surprised.

Piglet nodded.

"My present?"

Piglet nodded again.

"The balloon?"

"Yes."

"Thank you, Piglet," said Eeyore. "You don't mind my asking," he went on, "but what colour was this balloon when it—when it *was* a balloon?"

"Red."

"I just wondered. . . . Red," he murmured to himself. "My favourite colour. . . . How big was it?"

"About as big as me."

"I just wondered. . . . About as big as Piglet," he said to himself sadly. "My favourite size. Well, well."

Piglet felt very miserable, and didn't know what to say. He was still opening his mouth to begin something, and then deciding that it wasn't any good saying *that*, when he heard a shout from the other side of the river, and there was Pooh.

"Many happy returns of the day," called out Pooh, forgetting that he had said it already.

"Thank you, Pooh, I'm having them," said Eeyore gloomily.

"I've brought you a little present," said Pooh excitedly.

"I've had it," said Eeyore.

Pooh had now splashed across the stream to Eeyore, and Piglet was sitting a little way off, his head in his paws, snuffling to himself.

"It's a Useful Pot," said Pooh. "Here it is. And it's got 'A Very Happy Birthday with love from Pooh' written on it. That's what all that writing is. And it's for putting things in. There!"

When Eeyore saw the pot, he became quite excited.

"Why!" he said. "I believe my Balloon will just go into that Pot!"

"Oh, no, Eeyore," said Pooh. "Balloons are much too big to go into Pots. What you do with a balloon is, you hold the balloon—"

"Not mine," said Eeyore proudly. "Look, Piglet!" And as Piglet looked sorrowfully round, Eeyore picked the balloon up with his teeth, and placed it carefully in the pot; picked it out and put it on the ground; and then picked it up again and put it carefully back.

"So it does!" said Pooh. "It goes in!"

"So it does!" said Piglet. "And it comes out!"

"Doesn't it?" said Eeyore. "It goes in and out like anything."

"I'm very glad," said Pooh happily, "that I thought of giving you a Useful Pot to put things in."

"I'm very glad," said Piglet happily, "that I thought of giving you Something to put in a Useful Pot."

But Eeyore wasn't listening. He was taking the balloon out, and putting it back again, as happy as could be. . . .

"And didn't *I* give him anything?" asked Christopher Robin sadly.

"Of course you did," I said. "You gave him—don't you remember—a little—a little—"

"I gave him a box of paints to paint things with."

"That was it."

"Why didn't I give it to him in the morning?"

"You were so busy getting his party ready for him. He had a cake with icing on the top, and three candles, and his name in pink sugar, and—"

"Yes, *I* remember," said Christopher Robin.

CHAPTER VII

In Which

Kanga and Baby Roo Come to the Forest,

and Piglet Has a Bath

Nobody seemed to know where they came from, but there they were in the Forest: Kanga and Baby Roo. When Pooh asked Christopher Robin, "How did they come here?" Christopher Robin said, "In the Usual Way, if you know what I mean, Pooh," and Pooh, who didn't, said "Oh!" Then he nodded his head twice and said, "In the Usual Way. Ah!" Then he went to call upon his friend Piglet to see what *he* thought about it. And at Piglet's house he found Rabbit. So they all talked about it together.

"What I don't like about it is this," said Rabbit. "Here are we—you, Pooh, and you, Piglet, and Me—and suddenly—"

"And Eeyore," said Pooh.

"And Eeyore—and then suddenly—"

"And Owl," said Pooh.

"And Owl—and then all of a sudden—"

"Oh, and Eeyore," said Pooh. "I was forgetting *him*."

"Here—we—are," said Rabbit very slowly and carefully, "all—of—us, and then, suddenly, we wake up one morning and, what do we find? We find a Strange Animal among us. An animal of whom we have never even heard before! An animal who carries her family about with her in her pocket! Suppose *I* carried *my* family about with me in *my* pocket, how many pockets should I want?"

"Sixteen," said Piglet.

"Seventeen, isn't it?" said Rabbit. "And one more for a handkerchief—that's eighteen. Eighteen pockets in one suit! I haven't time."

There was a long and thoughtful silence . . . and then Pooh, who had been frowning very hard for some minutes, said: "*I* make it fifteen."

"What?" said Rabbit.

"Fifteen."

"Fifteen what?"

"Your family."

"What about them?"

Pooh rubbed his nose and said that he thought Rabbit had been talking about his family.

"Did I?" said Rabbit carelessly.

"Yes, you said—"

"Never mind, Pooh," said Piglet impatiently.

"The question is, What are we to do about Kanga?"

"Oh, I see," said Pooh.

"The best way," said Rabbit, "would be this. The best way would be to steal Baby Roo and hide him, and then when Kanga says, 'Where's Baby Roo?' we say, '*Aha!*'"

"*Aha!*" said Pooh, practising. "*Aha! Aha!* . . . Of course," he went on, "we could say 'Aha!' even if we hadn't stolen Baby Roo."

"Pooh," said Rabbit kindly, "you haven't any brain."

"I know," said Pooh humbly.

"We say '*Aha!*' so that Kanga knows that *we* know where Baby Roo is. '*Aha!*' means 'We'll tell you where Baby Roo is, if you promise to go away from the Forest and never come back.' Now don't talk while I think."

Pooh went into a corner and tried saying "Aha!" in that sort of voice. Sometimes it seemed to him that it did mean what Rabbit said, and sometimes it seemed to him that it didn't. "I suppose it's just practice," he thought. "I wonder if Kanga will have to practise too so as to understand it."

"There's just one thing," said Piglet, fidgeting a bit. "I was talking to Christopher Robin, and he said that a Kanga was Generally Regarded as One of the Fiercer Animals. I am not frightened of Fierce Animals in the ordinary way, but it is well known that, if One of the Fiercer Animals is Deprived of Its Young, it becomes as fierce as Two of the Fiercer Animals. In which case '*Aha!*' is perhaps a *foolish* thing to say."

"Piglet," said Rabbit, taking out a pencil, and licking the end of it, "you haven't any pluck."

"It is hard to be brave," said Piglet, sniffing slightly, "when you're only a Very Small Animal."

Rabbit, who had begun to write very busily, looked up and said:

"It is because you are a very small animal that you will be Useful in the adventure before us."

Piglet was so excited at the idea of being Useful that he forgot to be frightened any more, and when Rabbit went on to say that Kangas were only Fierce during the winter months, being at other times of an Affectionate Disposition, he could hardly sit still, he was so eager to begin being useful at once.

"What about me?" said Pooh sadly. "I suppose *I* shan't be useful?"

"Never mind, Pooh," said Piglet comfortingly. "Another time perhaps."

"Without Pooh," said Rabbit solemnly as he sharpened his pencil, "the adventure would be impossible."

"Oh!" said Piglet, and tried not to look disappointed. But Pooh went into a corner of the room and said proudly to himself, "Impossible without Me! *That* sort of Bear."

"Now listen all of you," said Rabbit when he had finished writing, and Pooh and Piglet sat listening very eagerly with their mouths open. This was what Rabbit read out:

PLAN TO CAPTURE BABY ROO

1. *General Remarks.* Kanga runs faster than any of Us, even Me.

2. *More General Remarks.* Kanga never takes her eye off Baby Roo, except when he's safely buttoned up in her pocket.

3. *Therefore.* If we are to capture Baby Roo, we must get a Long Start, because Kanga runs faster than any of Us, even Me. (*See* 1.)

4. *A Thought.* If Roo had jumped out of Kanga's pocket and Piglet had jumped in, Kanga wouldn't know the difference, because Piglet is a Very Small Animal.

5. Like Roo.

6. But Kanga would have to be looking the other way first, so as not to see Piglet jumping in.

7. See 2.

8. *Another Thought.* But if Pooh was talking to her very excitedly, she *might* look the other way for a moment.

9. And then I could run away with Roo.

10. Quickly.

11. *And Kanga wouldn't discover the difference until Afterwards.*

Well, Rabbit read this out proudly, and for a little while after he had read it nobody said anything. And then Piglet, who had been opening and shutting his mouth without making any noise, managed to say very huskily:

"And—Afterwards?"

"How do you mean?"

"When Kanga *does* Discover the Difference?"

"Then we all say '*Aha!*'"

"All three of us?"

"Yes."

"Oh!"

"Why, what's the trouble, Piglet?"

"Nothing," said Piglet, "as long as *we all three* say it. As long as we all three say it," said Piglet, "I don't mind," he said, "but I shouldn't care to say '*Aha!*' by myself. It wouldn't sound *nearly* so well. By the way," he said, "you *are* quite sure about what you said about the winter months?"

"The winter months?"

"Yes, only being Fierce in the Winter Months."

"Oh, yes, yes, that's all right. Well, Pooh? You see what you have to do?"

"No," said Pooh Bear. "Not yet," he said. "What *do* I do?"

"Well, you just have to talk very hard to Kanga so as she doesn't notice anything."

"Oh! What about?"

"Anything you like."

"You mean like telling her a little bit of poetry or something?"

"That's it," said Rabbit. "Splendid. Now come along."

So they all went out to look for Kanga.

Kanga and Roo were spending a quiet afternoon in a sandy part of the Forest. Baby Roo was practising very small jumps in the sand, and falling down mouse-holes and climbing out of them, and Kanga was fidgeting about and saying, "Just one more jump, dear, and then we must go home." And at that moment who should come stumping up the hill but Pooh.

"Good afternoon, Kanga."

"Good afternoon, Pooh."

"Look at me jumping," squeaked Roo, and fell into another mouse-hole.

"Hallo, Roo, my little fellow!"

"We were just going home," said Kanga. "Good afternoon, Rabbit. Good afternoon, Piglet."

Rabbit and Piglet, who had now come up from the other side of the hill, said, "Good afternoon," and "Hallo, Roo," and Roo asked them to look at him jumping, so they stayed and looked.

And Kanga looked too. . . .

"Oh, Kanga," said Pooh, after Rabbit had winked at him twice, "I don't know if you are interested in Poetry at all?"

"Hardly at all," said Kanga.

"Oh!" said Pooh.

"Roo, dear, just one more jump and then we must go home."

There was a short silence while Roo fell down another mouse-hole.

"Go on," said Rabbit in a loud whisper behind his paw.

"Talking of Poetry," said Pooh, "I made up a little piece as I was coming along. It went like this. Er—now let me see—"

"Fancy!" said Kanga. "Now Roo, dear—"

"You'll like this piece of poetry," said Rabbit.

"You'll love it," said Piglet.

"You must listen very carefully," said Rabbit.

"So as not to miss any of it," said Piglet.

"Oh, yes," said Kanga, but she still looked at Baby Roo.

"*How* did it go, Pooh?" said Rabbit.

Pooh gave a little cough and began.

LINES WRITTEN BY A BEAR OF VERY LITTLE BRAIN

On Monday, when the sun is hot
I wonder to myself a lot:
"Now is it true, or is it not,
"That what is which and which is what?"

On Tuesday, when it hails and snows,
The feeling on me grows and grows
That hardly anybody knows
If those are these or these are those.

On Wednesday, when the sky is blue,
And I have nothing else to do,
I sometimes wonder if it's true
That who is what and what is who.

On Thursday, when it starts to freeze
And hoar-frost twinkles on the trees,
How very readily one sees
That these are whose—but whose are these?

On Friday—

"Yes, it is, isn't it?" said Kanga, not waiting to hear what
happened on Friday. "Just one more jump, Roo, dear, and
then we really *must* be going."

Rabbit gave Pooh a hurrying-up sort of nudge.

"Talking of Poetry," said Pooh quickly, "have you ever noticed that tree right over there?"

"Where?" said Kanga. "Now, Roo—"

"Right over there," said Pooh, pointing behind Kanga's back.

"No," said Kanga. "Now jump in, Roo, dear, and we'll go home."

"You ought to look at that tree right over there," said Rabbit. "Shall I lift you in, Roo?" And he picked up Roo in his paws.

"I can see a bird in it from here," said Pooh. "Or is it a fish?"

"You ought to see that bird from here," said Rabbit. "Unless it's a fish."

"It isn't a fish, it's a bird," said Piglet.

"So it is," said Rabbit.

"Is it a starling or a blackbird?" said Pooh.

"That's the whole question," said Rabbit. "Is it a blackbird or a starling?"

And then at last Kanga did turn her head to look. And the moment that her head was turned, Rabbit said in a loud voice "In you go, Roo!" and in jumped Piglet into Kanga's pocket, and off scampered Rabbit, with Roo in his paws, as fast as he could.

"Why, where's Rabbit?" said Kanga, turning round again. "Are you all right, Roo, dear?"

Piglet made a squeaky Roo-noise from the bottom of Kanga's pocket.

"Rabbit had to go away," said Pooh. "I think he thought of something he had to go and see about suddenly."

"And Piglet?"

"I think Piglet thought of something at the same time. Suddenly."

"Well, we must be getting home," said Kanga. "Goodbye, Pooh." And in three large jumps she was gone.

Pooh looked after her as she went.

"I wish I could jump like that," he thought. "Some can and some can't. That's how it is."

But there were moments when Piglet wished that Kanga couldn't. Often, when he had had a long walk home through the Forest, he had wished that he were a bird; but now he thought jerkily to himself at the bottom of Kanga's pocket,

this   take

"If   is   shall   really   to

flying I   never   it."

And as he went up in the air he said, "*Oooooo!*" and as he came down he said, "*Ow!*" And he was saying, "*Ooooooo-ow, Ooooooo-ow, Ooooooo-ow*" all the way to Kanga's house.

Of course as soon as Kanga unbuttoned her pocket, she saw what had happened. Just for a moment, she thought she was frightened, and then she knew she wasn't; for she felt quite sure that Christopher Robin would never let any harm happen to Roo. So she said to herself, "If they are having a joke with me, I will have a joke with them."

"Now then, Roo, dear," she said, as she took Piglet out of her pocket. "Bed-time."

"*Aha!*" said Piglet, as well as he could after his Terrifying Journey. But it wasn't a very good "*Aha!*" and Kanga didn't seem to understand what it meant.

"Bath first," said Kanga in a cheerful voice.

"*Aha!*" said Piglet again, looking round anxiously for the others. But the others weren't there. Rabbit was playing with Baby Roo in his own house, and feeling more fond of him every minute, and Pooh, who had decided to be a Kanga, was still at the sandy place on the top of the Forest, practising jumps.

"I am not at all sure," said Kanga in a thoughtful voice, "that it wouldn't be a good idea to have a *cold* bath this evening. Would you like that, Roo, dear?"

Piglet, who had never been really fond of baths, shuddered a long indignant shudder, and said in as brave a voice as he could:

"Kanga, I see that the time has come to speak plainly."

"Funny little Roo," said Kanga, as she got the bath-water ready.

"I am *not* Roo," said Piglet loudly. "I am Piglet!"

"Yes, dear, yes," said Kanga soothingly. "And imitating Piglet's voice too! So clever of him," she went on, as she took a large bar of yellow soap out of the cupboard. "What *will* he be doing next?"

"Can't you *see?*" shouted Piglet. "Haven't you got *eyes?* Look at me!"

"I *am* looking, Roo, dear," said Kanga rather severely. "And you know what I told you yesterday about making faces. If you go on making faces like Piglet's, you will grow up to *look* like Piglet—and *then* think how sorry you will be. Now then, into the bath, and don't let me have to speak to you about it again."

Before he knew where he was, Piglet was in the bath, and Kanga was scrubbing him firmly with a large lathery flannel.

"Ow!" cried Piglet. "Let me out! I'm Piglet!"

"Don't open the mouth, dear, or the soap goes in," said Kanga. "There! What did I tell you?"

"You—you—you did it on purpose," spluttered Piglet, as soon as he could speak again . . . and then accidentally had another mouthful of lathery flannel.

"That's right, dear, don't say anything," said Kanga, and in another minute Piglet was out of the bath, and being rubbed dry with a towel.

"Now," said Kanga, "there's your medicine, and then bed."

"W-w-what medicine?" said Piglet.

"To make you grow big and strong, dear. You don't want to grow up small and weak like Piglet, do you? Well, then!"

At that moment there was a knock at the door.

"Come in," said Kanga, and in came Christopher Robin.

"Christopher Robin, Christopher Robin!" cried Piglet. "Tell Kanga who I am! She keeps saying I'm Roo. I'm *not* Roo, am I?"

Christopher Robin looked at him very carefully, and shook his head.

"You can't be Roo," he said, "because I've just seen Roo playing in Rabbit's house."

"Well!" said Kanga. "Fancy that! Fancy my making a mistake like that."

"There you are!" said Piglet. "I told you so. I'm Piglet."

Christopher Robin shook his head again.

"Oh, you're not Piglet," he said. "I know Piglet well, and he's *quite* a different colour."

Piglet began to say that this was because he had just had a bath, and then he thought that perhaps he wouldn't say that, and as he opened his mouth to say something else, Kanga slipped the medicine spoon in, and then patted him on the back and told him that it was really quite a nice taste when you got used to it.

"I knew it wasn't Piglet," said Kanga. "I wonder who it can be."

"Perhaps it's some relation of Pooh's," said Christopher Robin. "What about a nephew or an uncle or something?"

Kanga agreed that this was probably what it was, and said that they would have to call it by some name.

"I shall call it Pootel," said Christopher Robin. "Henry Pootel for short."

And just when it was decided, Henry Pootel wriggled out of Kanga's arms and jumped to the ground. To his great joy Christopher Robin had left the door open. Never had Henry Pootel Piglet run so fast as he ran then, and he didn't stop running until he had got quite close to his house. But when he was a hundred yards away he stopped running, and rolled the rest of the way home, so as to get his own nice comfortable colour again. . . .

So Kanga and Roo stayed in the Forest. And every Tuesday Roo spent the day with his great friend Rabbit, and every Tuesday Kanga spent the day with her great friend Pooh, teaching him to jump, and every Tuesday Piglet spent the day with his great friend Christopher Robin. So they were all happy again.

CHAPTER VIII

In Which
Christopher Robin Leads an Expotition
to the North Pole

One fine day Pooh had stumped up to the top of the Forest to see if his friend Christopher Robin was interested in Bears at all. At breakfast that morning (a simple meal of marmalade spread lightly over a honeycomb or two) he had suddenly thought of a new song. It began like this:

"Sing Ho! for the life of a Bear!"

When he had got as far as this, he scratched his head, and thought to himself "That's a very good start for a song, but what about the second line?" He tried singing "Ho," two or three times, but it didn't seem to help. "Perhaps it would be better," he thought, "if I sang Hi for the life of a Bear." So he sang it . . . but it wasn't. "Very well, then," he said, "I shall sing that first line twice, and perhaps if I sing it very quickly, I shall find myself singing the third and fourth lines before I have time to think of them, and that will be a Good Song. Now then":

> Sing Ho! for the life of a Bear!
> Sing Ho! for the life of a Bear!
> I don't much mind if it rains or snows,
> 'Cos I've got a lot of honey on my nice new nose,
> I don't much care if it snows or thaws,
> 'Cos I've got a lot of honey on my nice clean paws!
> Sing Ho! for a Bear!
> Sing Ho! for a Pooh!
> And I'll have a little something in an hour or two!

He was so pleased with this song that he sang it all the way to the top of the Forest, "and if I go on singing it much longer," he thought, "it will be time for the little something, and then the last line won't be true." So he turned it into a hum instead.

Christopher Robin was sitting outside his door, putting on his Big Boots. As soon as he saw the Big Boots, Pooh knew that an Adventure was going to happen, and he brushed the honey off his nose with the back of his paw, and spruced himself up as well as he could, so as to look Ready for Anything.

"Good-morning, Christopher Robin," he called out.

"Hallo, Pooh Bear. I can't get this boot on."

"That's bad," said Pooh.

"Do you think you could very kindly lean against me, 'cos I keep pulling so hard that I fall over backwards."

Pooh sat down, dug his feet into the ground, and pushed hard against Christopher Robin's back, and Christopher Robin pushed hard against his, and pulled and pulled at his boot until he had got it on.

"And that's that," said Pooh. "What do we do next?"

"We are all going on an Expedition," said Christopher Robin, as he got up and brushed himself. "Thank you, Pooh."

"Going on an Expotition?" said Pooh eagerly. "I don't think I've ever been on one of those. Where are we going to on this Expotition?"

"Expedition, silly old Bear. It's got an 'x' in it."

"Oh!" said Pooh. "I know." But he didn't really.

"We're going to discover the North Pole."

"Oh!" said Pooh again. "What *is* the North Pole?" he asked.

"It's just a thing you discover," said Christopher Robin carelessly, not being quite sure himself.

"Oh! I see," said Pooh. "Are bears any good at discovering it?"

"Of course they are. And Rabbit and Kanga and all of you. It's an Expedition. That's what an Expedition means. A long line of everybody. You'd better tell the others to get ready, while I see if my gun's all right. And we must all bring Provisions."

"Bring what?"

"Things to eat."

"Oh!" said Pooh happily. "I thought you said Provisions. I'll go and tell them." And he stumped off.

The first person he met was Rabbit.

"Hallo, Rabbit," he said, "is that you?"

"Let's pretend it isn't," said Rabbit, "and see what happens."

"I've got a message for you."

"I'll give it to him."

"We're all going on an Expotition with Christopher Robin!"

"What is it when we're on it?"

"A sort of boat, I think," said Pooh.

"Oh! that sort."

"Yes. And we're going to discover a Pole or something. Or was it a Mole? Anyhow we're going to discover it."

"We are, are we?" said Rabbit.

"Yes. And we've got to bring Pro—things to eat with us. In case we want to eat them. Now I'm going down to Piglet's. Tell Kanga, will you?"

He left Rabbit and hurried down to Piglet's house. The

Piglet was sitting on the ground at the door of his house blowing happily at a dandelion, and wondering whether it would be this year, next year, sometime or never. He had just discovered that it would be never, and was trying to remember what "*it*" was, and hoping it wasn't anything nice, when Pooh came up.

"Oh! Piglet," said Pooh excitedly, "we're going on an Expotition, all of us, with things to eat. To discover something."

"To discover what?" said Piglet anxiously.

"Oh! just something."

"Nothing fierce?"

"Christopher Robin didn't say anything about fierce. He just said it had an 'x.' "

"It isn't their necks I mind," said Piglet earnestly. "It's their teeth. But if Christopher Robin is coming I don't mind anything."

In a little while they were all ready at the top of the Forest, and the Expotition started. First came Christopher Robin and Rabbit, then Piglet and Pooh; then Kanga, with Roo in her pocket, and Owl; then Eeyore; and, at the end, in a long line, all Rabbit's friends-and-relations.

"I didn't ask them," explained Rabbit carelessly. "They just came. They always do. They can march at the end, after Eeyore."

"What I say," said Eeyore, "is that it's unsettling. I didn't want to come on this Expo—what Pooh said. I only came to oblige. But here I am; and if I am the end of the Expo—what we're talking about—then let me *be* the end. But if, every time I want to sit down for a little rest, I have to brush away half a dozen of Rabbit's smaller friends-and-relations first, then this isn't an Expo—whatever it is—at all, it's simply a Confused Noise. That's what *I* say."

"I see what Eeyore means," said Owl. "If you ask me—"

"I'm not asking anybody," said Eeyore. "I'm just telling everybody. We can look for the North Pole, or we can play 'Here we go gathering Nuts and May' with the end part of an ant's nest. It's all the same to me."

There was a shout from the top of the line.

"Come on!" called Christopher Robin.

"Come on!" called Pooh and Piglet

"Come on!" called Owl.

"We're starting," said Rabbit. "I must go." And he hurried off to the front of the Expotition with Christopher Robin.

"All right," said Eeyore. "We're going. Only Don't Blame Me."

So off they all went to discover the Pole. And as they walked, they chattered to each other of this and that, all except Pooh, who was making up a song.

"This is the first verse," he said to Piglet, when he was ready with it.

"First verse of what?"

"My song."

"What song?"

"This one."

"Which one?"

"Well, if you listen, Piglet, you'll hear it."

"How do you know I'm not listening?"

Pooh couldn't answer that one, so he began to sing.

> They all went off to discover the Pole,
>> Owl and Piglet and Rabbit and all;
> It's a Thing you Discover, as I've been tole
>> By Owl and Piglet and Rabbit and all.
> Eeyore, Christopher Robin and Pooh
> And Rabbit's relations all went too—
> And where the Pole was none of them knew. . . .
>> Sing Hey! for Owl and Rabbit and all!

"Hush!" said Christopher Robin turning round to Pooh, "we're just coming to a Dangerous Place."

"Hush!" said Pooh turning round quickly to Piglet.

"Hush!" said Piglet to Kanga.

"Hush!" said Kanga to Owl, while Roo said "Hush!" several times to himself very quietly.

"Hush!" said Owl to Eeyore.

"*Hush!*" said Eeyore in a terrible voice to all Rabbit's friends-and-relations, and "Hush!" they said hastily to each other all down the line, until it got to the last one of all. And the last and smallest friend-and-relation was so upset to find that the whole Expotition was saying "Hush!" to *him*, that he buried himself head downwards in a crack in the ground, and stayed there for two days until the danger was over, and then went home in a great hurry, and lived quietly with his Aunt ever-afterwards. His name was Alexander Beetle.

They had come to a stream which twisted and tumbled between high rocky banks, and Christopher Robin saw at once how dangerous it was.

"It's just the place," he explained, "for an Ambush."

"What sort of bush?" whispered Pooh to Piglet. "A gorse-bush?"

"My dear Pooh," said Owl in his superior way, "don't you know what an Ambush is?"

"Owl," said Piglet, looking round at him severely, "Pooh's

whisper was a perfectly private whisper, and there was no need—"

"An Ambush," said Owl, "is a sort of Surprise."

"So is a gorse-bush sometimes," said Pooh.

"An Ambush, as I was about to explain to Pooh," said Piglet, "is a sort of Surprise."

"If people jump out at you suddenly, that's an Ambush," said Owl.

"It's an Ambush, Pooh, when people jump at you suddenly," explained Piglet.

Pooh, who now knew what an Ambush was, said that a gorse-bush had sprung at him suddenly one day when he fell off a tree, and he had taken six days to get all the prickles out of himself.

"We are not *talking* about gorse-bushes," said Owl a little crossly.

"I am," said Pooh.

They were climbing very cautiously up the stream now, going from rock to rock, and after they had gone a little way they came to a place where the banks widened out at each side, so that on each side of the water there was a level strip of grass on which they could sit down and rest. As soon as he saw this, Christopher Robin called "Halt!" and they all sat down and rested.

"I think," said Christopher Robin, "that we ought to eat

all our Provisions now, so that we shan't have so much to carry."

"Eat all our what?" said Pooh.

"All that we've brought," said Piglet, getting to work.

"That's a good idea," said Pooh, and he got to work too.

"Have you all got something?" asked Christopher Robin with his mouth full.

"All except me," said Eeyore. "As Usual." He looked round at them in his melancholy way. "I suppose none of you are sitting on a thistle by any chance?"

"I believe I am," said Pooh. "Ow!" He got up, and looked behind him. "Yes, I was. I thought so."

"Thank you, Pooh. If you've quite finished with it." He moved across to Pooh's place, and began to eat.

"It don't do them any Good, you know, sitting on them," he went on, as he looked up munching. "Takes all the Life out of them. Remember that another time, all of you. A little Consideration, a little Thought for Others, makes all the difference."

As soon as he had finished his lunch Christopher Robin whispered to Rabbit, and Rabbit said, "Yes, yes, of course," and they walked a little way up the stream together.

"I didn't want the others to hear," said Christopher Robin.

"Quite so," said Rabbit, looking important.

"It's—I wondered—It's only—Rabbit, I suppose *you* don't know, What does the North Pole *look* like?"

"Well," said Rabbit, stroking his whiskers. "Now you're asking me."

"I did know once, only I've sort of forgotten," said Christopher Robin carelessly.

"It's a funny thing," said Rabbit, "but I've sort of forgotten too, although I did know *once*."

"I suppose it's just a pole stuck in the ground?"

"Sure to be a pole," said Rabbit, "because of calling it a pole, and if it's a pole, well, I should think it would be sticking in the ground, shouldn't you, because there'd be nowhere else to stick it."

"Yes, that's what I thought."

"The only thing," said Rabbit, "is, *where is it sticking?*"

"That's what we're looking for," said Christopher Robin.

They went back to the others. Piglet was lying on his back, sleeping peacefully. Roo was washing his face and paws in the stream, while Kanga explained to everybody proudly that this was the first time he had ever washed his face himself, and Owl was telling Kanga an Interesting Anecdote full of long words like Encyclopædia and Rhododendron to which Kanga wasn't listening.

"I don't hold with all this washing," grumbled Eeyore. "This modern Behind-the-ears nonsense. What do *you* think, Pooh?"

"Well," said Pooh, "*I* think—"

But we shall never know what Pooh thought, for there came a sudden squeak from Roo, a splash, and a loud cry of alarm from Kanga.

"So much for *washing*," said Eeyore.

"Roo's fallen in!" cried Rabbit, and he and Christopher Robin came rushing down to the rescue.

"Look at me swimming!" squeaked Roo from the middle of his pool, and was hurried down a waterfall into the next pool.

"Are you all right, Roo dear?" called Kanga anxiously.

"Yes!" said Roo. "Look at me sw—" and down he went over the next waterfall into another pool.

Everybody was doing something to help. Piglet, wide awake suddenly, was jumping up and down and making "Oo, I say" noises; Owl was explaining that in a case of Sudden and Temporary Immersion the Important Thing was to keep the Head Above Water; Kanga was jumping along the bank, saying "Are you *sure* you're all right, Roo dear?" to which Roo, from whatever pool he was in at the moment, was answering "Look at me swimming!" Eeyore had turned round and hung his tail over the first pool into which Roo fell, and with his back to the accident was grumbling quietly to himself, and saying, "All this washing; but catch on to my tail, little Roo, and you'll be all right"; and, Christopher Robin and Rabbit came hurrying past Eeyore, and were calling out to the others in front of them.

"All right, Roo, I'm coming," called Christopher Robin.

"Get something across the stream lower down, some of you fellows," called Rabbit.

But Pooh was getting something. Two pools below Roo
he was standing with a long pole in his paws, and Kanga
came up and took one end of it, and between them they
held it across the lower part of the pool; and Roo, still bub-
bling proudly, "Look at me swimming," drifted up against
it, and climbed out.

"Did you see me swimming?" squeaked Roo excitedly,
while Kanga scolded him and rubbed him down. "Pooh,
did you see me swimming? That's called swimming, what
I was doing. Rabbit, did you see what I was doing? Swimming. Hallo, Piglet! I say, Piglet! What do you think I was
doing! Swimming! Christopher Robin, did you see me—"

But Christopher Robin wasn't listening. He was looking
at Pooh.

"Pooh," he said, "where did you find that pole?"

Pooh looked at the pole in his hands.

"I just found it," he said. "I thought it ought to be useful. I just picked it up."

"Pooh," said Christopher Robin solemnly, "the Expedition is over. You have found the North Pole!"

"Oh!" said Pooh.

Eeyore was sitting with his tail in the water when they all got back to him.

"Tell Roo to be quick, somebody," he said. "My tail's getting cold. I don't want to mention it, but I just mention it. I don't want to complain but there it is. My tail's cold."

"Here I am!" squeaked Roo.

"Oh, there you are."

"Did you see me swimming?"

Eeyore took his tail out of the water, and swished it from side to side.

"As I expected," he said. "Lost all feeling. Numbed it. That's what it's done. Numbed it. Well, as long as nobody minds, I suppose it's all right."

"Poor old Eeyore. I'll dry it for you," said Christopher Robin, and he took out his handkerchief and rubbed it up.

"Thank you, Christopher Robin. You're the only one who seems to understand about tails. They don't think— that's what the matter with some of these others. They've no imagination. A tail isn't a tail to *them*, it's just a Little Bit Extra at the back."

"Never mind, Eeyore," said Christopher Robin, rubbing his hardest. "Is *that* better?"

"It's feeling more like a tail perhaps. It Belongs again, if you know what I mean."

"Hullo, Eeyore," said Pooh, coming up to them with his pole.

"Hullo, Pooh. Thank you for asking, but I shall be able to use it again in a day or two."

"Use what?" said Pooh.

"What we are talking about."

"I wasn't talking about anything," said Pooh, looking puzzled.

"My mistake again. I thought you were saying how sorry you were about my tail, being all numb, and could you do anything to help?"

"No," said Pooh. "That wasn't me," he said. He thought for a little and then suggested helpfully, "Perhaps it was somebody else."

"Well, thank him for me when you see him."

Pooh looked anxiously at Christopher Robin.

"Pooh's found the North Pole," said Christopher Robin. "Isn't that lovely?"

Pooh looked modestly down.

"Is that it?" said Eeyore.

"Yes," said Christopher Robin.

"Is that what we were looking for?"

"Yes," said Pooh.

"Oh!" said Eeyore. "Well, anyhow—it didn't rain," he said.

They stuck the pole in the ground, and Christopher Robin tied a message on to it.

NORTH POLE

DISCOVERED BY POOH

POOH FOUND IT.

Then they all went home again. And I think, but I am not quite sure, that Roo had a hot bath and went straight to bed. But Pooh went back to his own house, and feeling very proud of what he had done, had a little something to revive himself.

135

CHAPTER IX

In Which

Piglet Is Entirely Surrounded by Water

It rained and it rained and it rained. Piglet told himself that never in all his life, and *he* was goodness knows *how* old—three, was it, or four?—never had he seen so much rain. Days and days and days.

"If only," he thought, as he looked out of the window, "I had been in Pooh's house, or Christopher Robin's house, or Rabbit's house when it began to rain, then I should have had Company all this time, instead of being here all alone, with nothing to do except wonder when it will stop." And he imagined himself with Pooh, saying, "Did you ever see such rain, Pooh?" and Pooh saying, "Isn't it *awful*, Piglet?" and Piglet saying, "I wonder how it is over Christopher Robin's way" and Pooh saying, "I should think poor old Rabbit is about flooded out by this time." It would have been jolly to talk like this, and really, it wasn't much good having anything exciting like floods, if you couldn't share them with somebody.

For it was rather exciting. The little dry ditches in which Piglet had nosed about so often had become streams, the little streams across which he had splashed were rivers, and the river, between whose steep banks they had played so happily, had sprawled out of its own bed and was taking up so much room everywhere, that Piglet was beginning to wonder whether it would be coming into *his* bed soon.

"It's a little Anxious," he said to himself, "to be a Very Small Animal Entirely Surrounded by Water. Christopher Robin and Pooh could escape by Climbing Trees, and Kanga could escape by Jumping, and Rabbit could escape by Burrowing, and Owl could escape by Flying, and Eeyore could escape by—by Making a Loud Noise Until Rescued, and here am I, surrounded by water and I can't do *anything*."

It went on raining, and every day the water got a little higher, until now it was nearly up to Piglet's window . . . and still he hadn't done anything.

"There's Pooh," he thought to himself. "Pooh hasn't much Brain, but he never comes to any harm. He does silly things and they turn out right. There's Owl. Owl hasn't exactly got Brain, but he Knows Things. He would know the Right Thing to Do when Surrounded by Water. There's Rabbit.

He hasn't Learnt in Books, but he can always Think of a Clever Plan. There's Kanga. She isn't Clever, Kanga isn't, but she would be so anxious about Roo that she would do

a Good Thing to Do without thinking about It. And then there's Eeyore. And Eeyore is so miserable anyhow that he wouldn't mind about this. But I wonder what Christopher Robin would do?"

Then suddenly he remembered a story which Christopher Robin had told him about a man on a desert island who had written something in a bottle and thrown it in the sea; and Piglet thought that if he wrote something in a bottle and threw it in the water, perhaps somebody would come and rescue *him*!

He left the window and began to search his house, all of it that wasn't under water, and at last he found a pencil and a small piece of dry paper, and a bottle with a cork to it. And he wrote on one side of the paper:

HELP!

PIGLET   (ME)

and on the other side:

IT'S ME PIGLET, HELP HELP.

Then he put the paper in the bottle, and he corked the bottle up as tightly as he could, and he leant out of his window as far as he could lean without falling in, and he threw the bottle as far as he could throw—*splash!*—and in a little while it bobbed up again on the water; and he watched it floating slowly away in the distance, until his eyes ached with looking, and sometimes he thought it was the bottle, and sometimes he thought it was just a ripple on the water which he was following, and then suddenly he knew that he would never see it again and that he had done all that he could do to save himself.

"So now," he thought, "somebody else will have to do something, and I hope they will do it soon, because if they

don't I shall have to swim, which I can't, so I hope they do it soon." And then he gave a very long sigh and said, "I wish Pooh were here. It's so much more friendly with two."

When the rain began Pooh was asleep. It rained, and it rained, and it rained, and he slept and he slept and he slept. He had had a tiring day. You remember how he discovered the North Pole; well, he was so proud of this that he asked Christopher Robin if there were any other Poles such as a Bear of Little Brain might discover.

"There's a South Pole," said Christopher Robin, "and I expect there's an East Pole and a West Pole, though people don't like talking about them."

Pooh was very excited when he heard this, and suggested that they should have an Expotition to discover the East Pole, but Christopher Robin had thought of something else to do with Kanga; so Pooh went out to discover the East Pole by himself. Whether he discovered it or not, I forget; but he was so tired when he got home that, in the very middle of his supper, after he had been eating for little more than half-an-hour, he fell fast asleep in his chair, and slept and slept and slept.

Then suddenly he was dreaming. He was at the East Pole, and it was a very cold pole with the coldest sort of snow and ice all over it. He had found a bee-hive to sleep in, but there wasn't room for his legs, so he had left them outside. And Wild Woozles, such as inhabit the East Pole, came and nibbled all the fur off his legs to make nests for their Young. And the more they nibbled, the colder his legs got, until suddenly he woke up with an *Ow!*—and there he was, sitting in his chair with his feet in the water, and water all round him!

He splashed to his door and looked out. . . .

"This is Serious," said Pooh. "I must have an Escape."

So he took his largest pot of honey and escaped with it to a broad branch of his tree, well above the water, and then he climbed down again and escaped with another pot . . . and when the whole Escape was finished, there was Pooh sitting on his branch, dangling his legs, and there, beside him, were ten pots of honey. . . .

Two days later, there was Pooh, sitting on his branch, dangling his legs, and there, beside him, were four pots of honey. . . .

Three days later, there was Pooh, sitting on his branch, dangling his legs, and there, beside him, was one pot of honey.

Four days later, there was Pooh. . . .

And it was on the morning of the fourth day that Piglet's bottle came floating past him, and with one loud cry of "Honey!" Pooh plunged into the water, seized the bottle, and struggled back to his tree again.

"Bother!" said Pooh, as he opened it. "All that wet for nothing. What's that bit of paper doing?"

He took it out and looked at it.

"It's a Missage," he said to himself, "that's what it is. And that letter is a 'P,' and so is that, and so is that, and 'P' means 'Pooh,' so it's a very important Missage to me, and

I can't read it. I must find Christopher Robin or Owl or Piglet, one of those Clever Readers who can read things, and they will tell me what this message means. Only I can't swim. Bother!"

Then he had an idea, and I think that for a Bear of Very Little Brain, it was a good idea. He said to himself:

"If a bottle can float, then a jar can float, and if a jar floats, I can sit on the top of it, if it's a very big jar."

So he took his biggest jar, and corked it up. "All boats have to have a name," he said, "so I shall call mine *The*

Floating Bear." And with these words he dropped his boat into the water and jumped in after it.

For a little while Pooh and *The Floating Bear* were uncertain as to which of them was meant to be on the top, but

after trying one or two different positions, they settled down with *The Floating Bear* underneath and Pooh triumphantly astride it, paddling vigorously with his feet.

144

Christopher Robin lived at the very top of the Forest. It rained, and it rained, and it rained, but the water

couldn't come up to *his* house. It was rather jolly to look down into the valleys and see the water all round him, but it rained so hard that he stayed indoors most of the time, and thought about things. Every morning he went

out with his umbrella and put a stick in the place where the water came up to, and every next morning he went out and couldn't see his stick any more, so he put another stick in the place where the water came up to, and then he walked home again, and each morning he had a shorter way to walk than he had had the morning before. On the morning of the fifth day he saw the water all round him, and knew that for the first time in his life he was on a real island. Which was very exciting.

It was on this morning that Owl came flying over the water to say "How do you do," to his friend Christopher Robin.

"I say, Owl," said Christopher Robin, "isn't this fun? I'm on an island!"

"The atmospheric conditions have been very unfavourable lately," said Owl.

"The what?"

"It has been raining," explained Owl.

"Yes," said Christopher Robin. "It has."

"The flood-level has reached an unprecedented height."

"The who?"

"There's a lot of water about," explained Owl.

"Yes," said Christopher Robin, "there is."

"However, the prospects are rapidly becoming more favourable. At any moment—"

"Have you seen Pooh?"

"No. At any moment—"

"I hope he's all right," said Christopher Robin. "I've been wondering about him. I expect Piglet's with him. Do you think they're all right, Owl?"

"I expect so. You see, at any moment—"

"Do go and see, Owl. Because Pooh hasn't got very much brain, and he might do something silly, and I do love him so, Owl. Do you see, Owl?"

"That's all right," said Owl. "I'll go. Back directly." And he flew off.

In a little while he was back again.

"Pooh isn't there," he said.

"Not there?"

"Has *been* there. He's been sitting on a branch of his tree outside his house with nine pots of honey. But he isn't there now."

"Oh, Pooh!" cried Christopher Robin. "Where *are* you?"

"Here I am," said a growly voice behind him.

"Pooh!"

They rushed into each other's arms.

"How did you get here, Pooh?" asked Christopher Robin, when he was ready to talk again.

"On my boat," said Pooh proudly. "I had a Very Important Missage sent me in a bottle, and owing to having got some water in my eyes, I couldn't read it, so I brought it to you. On my boat."

With these proud words he gave Christopher Robin the missage.

"But it's from Piglet!" cried Christopher Robin when he had read it.

"Isn't there anything about Pooh in it?" asked Bear, looking over his shoulder.

Christopher Robin read the message aloud.

"Oh, are those 'P's' Piglets? I thought they were Poohs."

"We must rescue him at once! I thought he was with *you*, Pooh. Owl, could you rescue him on your back?"

"I don't think so," said Owl, after grave thought. "It is doubtful if the necessary dorsal muscles—"

"Then would you fly to him at *once* and say that Rescue is Coming? And Pooh and I will think of a Rescue and come as quick as ever we can. Oh, don't *talk*, Owl, go on quick!" And, still thinking of something to say, Owl flew off.

"Now then, Pooh," said Christopher Robin, "where's your boat?"

"I ought to say," explained Pooh as they walked down to the shore of the island, "that it isn't just an ordinary sort of boat. Sometimes it's a Boat, and sometimes it's more of an Accident. It all depends."

"Depends on what?"

"On whether I'm on the top of it or underneath it."

"Oh! Well, where is it?"

"There!" said Pooh, pointing proudly to *The Floating Bear*.

It wasn't what Christopher Robin expected, and the more he looked at it, the more he thought what a Brave and Clever Bear Pooh was, and the more Christopher Robin thought this, the more Pooh looked modestly down his nose and tried to pretend he wasn't.

"But it's too small for two of us," said Christopher Robin sadly.

"Three of us with Piglet."

"That makes it smaller still. Oh, Pooh Bear, what shall we do?"

And then this Bear, Pooh Bear, Winnie-the-Pooh, F.O.P. (Friend of Piglet's), R.C. (Rabbit's Companion), P.D. (Pole Discoverer), E.C. and T.F. (Eeyore's Comforter and Tail-finder)—in fact, Pooh himself—said something so clever that Christopher Robin could only look at him with mouth open and eyes staring, wondering if this was really the Bear of Very Little Brain whom he had known and loved so long.

"We might go in your umbrella," said Pooh.

"?"

"We might go in your umbrella," said Pooh.

"? ?"

"We might go in your umbrella," said Pooh.

"!!!!!"

For suddenly Christopher Robin saw that they might. He opened his umbrella and put it point downwards in the water. It floated but wobbled. Pooh got in. He was just

beginning to say that it was all right now, when he found that it wasn't, so after a short drink which he didn't really want he waded back to Christopher Robin. Then they both got in together, and it wobbled no longer.

"I shall call this boat *The Brain of Pooh*," said Christopher Robin, and *The Brain of Pooh* set sail forthwith in a southwesterly direction, revolving gracefully.

You can imagine Piglet's joy when at last the ship came in sight of him. In after-years he liked to think that he had been in Very Great Danger during the Terrible Flood, but the only danger he had really been in was in the last half-hour of his imprisonment, when Owl, who had just flown up, sat on a branch of his tree to comfort him, and told him a very long story about an aunt who had once laid a seagull's egg by mistake, and the story went on and on, rather like this sentence, until Piglet who was listening out of his window without much hope, went to sleep quietly and naturally, slipping slowly out of the window towards the water until he was only hanging on by his toes, at which moment luckily, a sudden loud squawk from Owl, which was really part of the story, being what his aunt said, woke the Piglet up and just gave him time to jerk himself back into safety and say, "How interesting, and did she?" when—well, you can imagine his joy when at last he saw the good ship, *The Brain of Pooh* (*Captain*, C. Robin; *1st Mate*, P. Bear)

coming over the sea to rescue him. Christopher Robin and Pooh again. . . .

And that is really the end of the story, and I am very tired after that last sentence, I think I shall stop there.

CHAPTER X

In Which
Christopher Robin Gives Pooh a Party,
and We Say Good-bye

One day when the sun had come back over the Forest, bringing with it the scent of May, and all the streams of the Forest were tinkling happily to find themselves their own pretty shape again, and the little pools lay dreaming of the life they had seen and the big things they had done, and in the warmth and quiet of the Forest the cuckoo was trying over his voice carefully and listening to see if he liked it, and wood-pigeons were complaining gently to themselves in their lazy comfortable way that it was the other fellow's fault, but it didn't matter very much; on such a day as this Christopher Robin whistled in a special way he had, and Owl came flying out of the Hundred Acre Wood to see what was wanted.

"Owl," said Christopher Robin, "I am going to give a party."

"You are, are you?" said Owl.

"And it's to be a special sort of party, because it's because of what Pooh did when he did what he did to save Piglet from the flood."

"Oh, that's what it's for, is it?" said Owl.

"Yes, so will you tell Pooh as quickly as you can, and all the others, because it will be tomorrow."

"Oh, it will, will it?" said Owl, still being as helpful as possible.

"So will you go and tell them, Owl?"

Owl tried to think of something very wise to say, but couldn't, so he flew off to tell the others. And the first person he told was Pooh.

"Pooh," he said, "Christopher Robin is giving a party."

"Oh!" said Pooh. And then seeing that Owl expected him to say something else, he said, "Will there be those little cake things with pink sugar icing?"

Owl felt that it was rather beneath him to talk about little cake things with pink sugar icing, so he told Pooh exactly what Christopher Robin had said, and flew off to Eeyore.

"A party for Me?" thought Pooh to himself. "How grand!" And he began to wonder if all the other animals would know that it was a special Pooh Party, and if Christopher Robin had told them about *The Floating Bear* and *The Brain of Pooh* and all the wonderful ships he had invented and sailed on, and he began to think how awful it would be if everybody had forgotten about it, and nobody quite knew what the party was for; and the more he thought like this, the more the party got muddled in his mind, like a dream when

nothing goes right. And the dream began to sing itself over in his head until it became a sort of song. It was an

ANXIOUS POOH SONG.

3 Cheers for Pooh!
(*For Who?*)
For Pooh—
(*Why what did he do?*)
I thought you knew;
He saved his friend from a wetting!
3 Cheers for Bear!
(*For where?*)
For Bear—
He couldn't swim,
But he rescued him!
(*He rescued who?*)
Oh, listen, do!

I am talking of Pooh—
(*Of who?*)
Of Pooh!
(*I'm sorry I keep forgetting*).
Well, Pooh was a Bear of Enormous Brain
(*Just say it again!*)
Of enormous brain—
(*Of enormous what?*)
Well, he ate a lot,
And I don't know if he could swim or not,
But he managed to float
On a sort of boat
(*On a sort of what?*)
Well, a sort of pot—
So now let's give him three hearty cheers
(*So now let's give him three hearty whiches?*)
And hope he'll be with us for years and years,
And grow in health and wisdom and riches!
3 Cheers for Pooh!
(*For who?*)
For Pooh—
3 Cheers for Bear!
(*For where?*)
For Bear—
3 Cheers for the wonderful Winnie-the-Pooh!
(*Just tell me, somebody—*WHAT DID HE DO?)

While this was going on inside him, Owl was talking to Eeyore.

"Eeyore," said Owl, "Christopher Robin is giving a party."

"Very interesting," said Eeyore. "I suppose they will be sending me down the odd bits which got trodden on. Kind and Thoughtful. Not at all, don't mention it."

"There is an Invitation for you."

"What's that like?"

"An Invitation!"

"Yes, I heard you. Who dropped it?"

"This isn't anything to eat, it's asking you to the party. Tomorrow."

Eeyore shook his head slowly.

"You mean Piglet. The little fellow with the excited ears. That's Piglet. I'll tell him."

"No, no!" said Owl, getting quite fussy. "It's you!"

"Are you sure?"

"Of course I'm sure. Christopher Robin said 'All of them! Tell all of them.' "

"All of them, except Eeyore?"

"All of them," said Owl sulkily.

"Ah!" said Eeyore. "A mistake, no doubt, but still, I shall come. Only don't blame *me* if it rains."

But it didn't rain. Christopher Robin had made a long table out of some long pieces of wood, and they all sat around it. Christopher Robin sat at one end, and Pooh sat at the other, and between them on one side were Owl and Eeyore and Piglet, and between them on the other side were Rabbit, and Roo and Kanga. And all Rabbit's friends and relations spread themselves about on the grass, and waited hopefully in case anybody spoke to them, or dropped anything, or asked them the time.

It was the first party to which Roo had ever been, and he was very excited. As soon as ever they had sat down he began to talk.

"Hallo, Pooh!" he squeaked.

"Hallo, Roo!" said Pooh.

Roo jumped up and down in his seat for a little while and then began again.

"Hallo, Piglet!" he squeaked.

Piglet waved a paw at him, being too busy to say anything.

"Hallo, Eeyore!" said Roo.

Eeyore nodded gloomily at him. "It will rain soon, you see if it doesn't," he said.

Roo looked to see if it didn't, and it didn't, so he said "Hallo, Owl!"—and Owl said "Hallo, my little fellow," in a kindly way, and went on telling Christopher Robin about an accident which had nearly happened to a friend of his whom Christopher Robin didn't know, and Kanga said to Roo, "Drink up your milk first, dear, and talk afterwards."

So Roo, who was drinking his milk, tried to say that he could do both at once . . . and had to be patted on the back and dried for quite a long time afterwards.

When they had all nearly eaten enough, Christopher Robin banged on the table with his spoon, and everybody stopped talking and was very silent, except Roo who was just finishing a loud attack of hiccups and trying to look as if it was one of Rabbit's relations.

"This party," said Christopher Robin, "is a party because of what someone did, and we all know who it was, and it's his party, because of what he did, and I've got a present for him and here it is." Then he felt about a little and whispered, "Where is it?"

While he was looking, Eeyore coughed in an impressive way and began to speak.

"Friends," he said, "including oddments, it is a great pleasure, or perhaps I had better say it has been a pleasure so far, to see you at my party. What I did was nothing. Any of you—except Rabbit and Owl and Kanga—would have done the same. Oh, and Pooh. My remarks do not, of course, apply to Piglet and Roo, because they are too small. Any of you would have done the same. But it just happened to be Me. It was not, I need hardly say, with an idea of getting what Christopher Robin is looking for now"—and he put his front leg to his mouth and said in a loud whisper, "Try under the table"—"that I did what I did—but because I feel that we should all do what we can to help. I feel that we should all—"

"H—hup!" said Roo accidentally.

"Roo, dear!" said Kanga reproachfully.

"Was it me?" asked Roo, a little surprised.

"What's Eeyore talking about?" Piglet whispered to Pooh.

"I don't know," said Pooh rather dolefully.

"I thought this was *your* party."

"I thought it was *once*. But I suppose it isn't."

"I'd sooner it was yours than Eeyore's," said Piglet.

"So would I," said Pooh.

"H—hup!" said Roo again.

"AS—I—WAS—SAYING," said Eeyore loudly and sternly, "as I was saying when I was interrupted by various Loud Sounds, I feel that—"

"Here it is!" cried Christopher Robin excitedly. "Pass it down to silly old Pooh. It's for Pooh."

"For Pooh?" said Eeyore.

"Of course it is. The best bear in all the world."

"I might have known," said Eeyore. "After all, one can't complain. I have my friends. Somebody spoke to me only yesterday. And was it last week or the week before that Rabbit bumped into me and said 'Bother!' The Social Round. Always something going on."

Nobody was listening, for they were all saying "Open it, Pooh," "What is it, Pooh?" "I know what it is," "No,

you don't" and other helpful remarks of this sort. And of course Pooh was opening it as quickly as ever he could, but without cutting the string, because you never know when a bit of string might be Useful. At last it was undone.

When Pooh saw what it was, he nearly fell down, he was so pleased. It was a Special Pencil Case. There were pencils in it marked "B" for Bear, and pencils marked "HB" for Helping Bear, and pencils marked "BB" for Brave Bear. There was a knife for sharpening the pencils, and india-rubber for rubbing out anything which you had spelt wrong, and a ruler for ruling lines for the words to walk on, and inches marked on the ruler in case you wanted to know how many inches anything was, and Blue Pencils and Red Pencils and Green Pencils for saying special things in blue and red and green. And all these lovely things were in little pockets of their own in a Special Case which shut with a click when you clicked it. And they were all for Pooh.

"Oh!" said Pooh.

"Oh, Pooh!" said everybody else except Eeyore.

"Thank-you," growled Pooh.

But Eeyore was saying to himself, "This writing business. Pencils and what-not. Over-rated, if you ask me. Silly stuff. Nothing in it."

Later on, when they had all said "Good-bye" and "Thank-you" to Christopher Robin, Pooh and Piglet walked home thoughtfully together in the golden evening, and for a long time they were silent.

"When you wake up in the morning, Pooh," said Piglet at last, "what's the first thing you say to yourself?"

"What's for breakfast?" said Pooh. "What do *you* say, Piglet?"

"I say, I wonder what's going to happen exciting *today*?" said Piglet.

Pooh nodded thoughtfully.
"It's the same thing," he said.

"And what did happen?" asked Christopher Robin.
"When?"
"Next morning."
"I don't know."
"Could you think and tell me and Pooh sometime?"
"If you wanted it very much."

"Pooh does," said Christopher Robin.

He gave a deep sigh, picked his bear up by the leg and walked off to the door, trailing Winnie-the-Pooh behind him. At the door he turned and said "Coming to see me have my bath?"

"I might," I said.

"Was Pooh's pencil case any better than mine?"

"It was just the same," I said.

He nodded and went out . . . and in a moment I heard Winnie-the-Pooh— *bump, bump, bump*—going up the stairs behind him.

When We Were Very Young

Halfway Down

———•———

to

Just Before We Begin

At one time (but I have changed my mind now) I thought I was going to write a little Note at the top of each of these poems, in the manner of Mr. William Wordsworth, who liked to tell his readers where he was staying, and which of his friends he was walking with, and what he was thinking about, when the idea of writing his poem came to him. You will find some lines about a swan here, if you get as far as that, and I should have explained to you in the Note that Christopher Robin, who feeds this swan in the mornings, has given him the name of "Pooh." This is a very fine name for a swan, because, if you call him and he doesn't come (which is a thing swans are good at), then you can pretend that you were just saying "Pooh!" to show how little you wanted him. Well, I should have told you that there are six cows who come down to Pooh's lake every afternoon to drink, and of course they say "Moo" as they come. So I thought to myself one fine day, walking with my friend Christopher Robin, "Moo rhymes with Pooh! Surely there is a bit of poetry to be got out of that?" Well, then, I began to think about the swan on his lake; and at first I thought how lucky it was that his name was Pooh; and then I didn't think about that any more . . . and the poem came quite differently from what I intended . . . and all I can say for it now is that, if it hadn't been for Christopher Robin, I shouldn't have written it; which, indeed, is all I can say for any of the others. So this is why these verses go about together, because they are all friends of Christopher Robin; and if I left out one because it was not quite like the one before, then I should have to leave out the one before because it was not quite like the next, which would be disappointing for them.

Then there is another thing. You may wonder sometimes who is supposed to be saying the verses. Is it the Author, that strange but uninteresting person, or is it Christopher Robin, or some other boy or girl, or Nurse, or Hoo? If I had followed Mr. Wordsworth's plan I could have explained this each time; but, as it is, you will have to decide for yourselves. If you are not quite sure, then it is probably Hoo. I don't know if you have ever met Hoo, but he is one of those curious children who look four on Monday, and eight on Tuesday, and are really twenty-eight on Saturday, and you never know whether it is the day when he can pronounce his "r's." He had a great deal to do with these verses. In fact, you might almost say that this book is entirely the unaided work of Christopher Robin, Hoo, and Mr. Shepard, who drew the pictures. They have said "Thank you" politely to each other several times, and now they say it to you for taking them into your house. "Thank you so much for asking us. We've come."

A.A.M

Corner-of-the-Street

Down by the corner of the street,
   Where the three roads meet,
     And the feet
Of the people as they pass go "Tweet-tweet-tweet—"
Who comes tripping round the corner of the street?
   One pair of shoes which are Nurse's;
   One pair of slippers which are Percy's . . .
     Tweet! Tweet! Tweet!

Buckingham Palace

They're changing guard at Buckingham Palace—
Christopher Robin went down with Alice.
Alice is marrying one of the guard.
"A soldier's life is terrible hard,"

Says Alice.

They're changing guard at Buckingham Palace—
Christopher Robin went down with Alice.
We saw a guard in a sentry-box.
"One of the sergeants looks after their socks,"

Says Alice.

They're changing guard at Buckingham Palace—
Christopher Robin went down with Alice.
We looked for the King, but he never came.
"Well, God take care of him, all the same,"
                    Says Alice.

They're changing guard at Buckingham Palace—
Christopher Robin went down with Alice.
They've great big parties inside the grounds.
"I wouldn't be King for a hundred pounds,"
                    Says Alice.

They're changing guard at Buckingham Palace—
Christopher Robin went down with Alice.
A face looked out, but it wasn't the King's.
"He's much too busy a-signing things,"
                    Says Alice.

They're changing guard at Buckingham Palace—
Christopher Robin went down with Alice.
"Do you think the King knows all about *me*?"
"Sure to, dear, but it's time for tea,"
                    Says Alice.

Happiness

John had
Great Big
Waterproof
Boots on;
John had a
Great Big
Waterproof
Hat;
John had a
Great Big
Waterproof
Mackintosh—
And that
(Said John)
Is
That.

The Christening

What shall I call
   My dear little dormouse?
His eyes are small,
   But his tail is e-nor-mouse.

I sometimes call him Terrible John,
'Cos his tail goes on—
And on—
And on.
And I sometimes call him Terrible Jack,
'Cos his tail goes on to the end of his back.
And I sometimes call him Terrible James,
'Cos he says he likes me calling him names. . .

   But I think I shall call him Jim,
   'Cos I *am* so fond of him.

Puppy and I

I met a man as I went walking;
We got talking,
Man and I.
"Where are you going to, Man?" I said
(I said to the Man as he went by).
"Down to the village, to get some bread.
Will you come with me?" "No, not I."

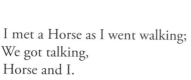

I met a Horse as I went walking;
We got talking,
Horse and I.
"Where are you going to, Horse, today?"
(I said to the Horse as he went by).
"Down to the village to get some hay.
Will you come with me?" "No, not I."

I met a Woman as I went walking;
We got talking,
Woman and I.
"Where are you going to, Woman, so early?"
(I said to the Woman as she went by).
"Down to the village to get some barley.
Will you come with me?" "No, not I."

I met some Rabbits as I went walking;
We got talking,
Rabbits and I.
"Where are you going in your brown fur coats?"
(I said to the Rabbits as they went by).
"Down to the village to get some oats.
Will you come with us?" "No, not I."

I met a Puppy as I went walking;
We got talking,
Puppy and I.
"Where are you going this nice fine day?"
(I said to the Puppy as he went by).
"Up in the hills to roll and play."
"*I'll* come with you, Puppy," said I.

Twinkletoes

When the sun
Shines through the leaves of the apple-tree,
When the sun
Makes shadows of the leaves of the apple-tree,
Then I pass
On the grass
From one leaf to another,
From one leaf to its brother,
Tip-toe, tip-toe!
Here I go!

The Four Friends

Ernest was an elephant, a great big fellow,
  Leonard was a lion with a six-foot tail,
George was a goat, and his beard was yellow,
    And James was a very small snail.

Leonard had a stall, and a great big strong one,
  Ernest had a manger, and its walls were thick,
George found a pen, but I think it was the wrong one,
    And James sat down on a brick.

Ernest started trumpeting, and cracked his manger,
   Leonard started roaring, and shivered his stall,
James gave the huffle of a snail in danger
      And nobody heard him at all.

Ernest started trumpeting and raised such a rumpus,
   Leonard started roaring and trying to kick,
James went a journey with the goat's new compass
      And he reached the end of his brick.

Ernest was an elephant and very well-intentioned,
   Leonard was a lion with a brave new tail,
George was a goat, as I think I have mentioned,
      But James was only a snail.

Lines and Squares

Whenever I walk in a London street,
I'm ever so careful to watch my feet;
   And I keep in the squares,
   And the masses of bears,
Who wait at the corners all ready to eat
The sillies who tread on the lines of the street,
   Go back to their lairs,
   And I say to them, "Bears,
   Just look how I'm walking in all of the squares!"

And the little bears growl to each other, "He's mine,
As soon as he's silly and steps on a line."
And some of the bigger bears try to pretend
That they came round the corner to look for a friend;
And they try to pretend that nobody cares
Whether you walk on the lines or squares.
But only the sillies believe their talk;
It's ever so portant how you walk.
And it's ever so jolly to call out, "Bears,
Just watch me walking in all the squares!"

Brownie

In a corner of the bedroom is a great big curtain,
  Someone lives behind it, but I don't know who;
I think it is a Brownie, but I'm not quite certain.
  (Nanny isn't certain, too.)

I looked behind the curtain, but he went so quickly—
  Brownies never wait to say, "How do you do?"
They wriggle off at once because they're all so tickly.
  (Nanny says they're tickly too.)

Independence

I nevcr did, I never did, I never *did* like
   "Now take care, dear!"
   I never did, I never did, I never *did* want
   "Hold-my-hand";
I never did, I never did, I never *did* think much of
   "Not up there, dear!"
   It's no good saying it. They don't understand.

Nursery Chairs

One of the chairs is South America,
One of the chairs is a ship at sea,
One is a cage for a great big lion,
And one is a chair for Me.

THE FIRST CHAIR

When I go up the Amazon,
I stop at night and fire a gun
　To call my faithful band.
And Indians in twos and threes,
Come silently between the trees,
　And wait for me to land.
And if I do not want to play
With any Indians today,
　I simply wave my hand.
And then they turn and go away—
　They always understand.

THE SECOND CHAIR

I'm a great big lion in my cage,
    And I often frighten Nanny with a roar.
      Then I hold her very tight, and
      Tell her not to be so frightened—
    And she doesn't be so frightened any more.

THE THIRD CHAIR

When I am in my ship, I see
 The other ships go sailing by.
A sailor leans and calls to me
 As his ship goes sailing by.
Across the sea he leans to me,
 Above the winds I hear him cry:
"Is this the way to Round-the-World?"
 He calls as he goes by.

THE FOURTH CHAIR

Whenever I sit in a high chair
   For breakfast or dinner or tea,
I try to pretend that it's *my* chair,
   And that I am a baby of three.

Shall I go off to South America?
   Shall I put out in my ship to sea?
Or get in my cage and be lions and tigers?
   Or—shall I be only Me?

Market Square

I had a penny,
A bright new penny,
I took my penny
   To the market square.
I wanted a rabbit,
A little brown rabbit,
And I looked for a rabbit
   'Most everywhere.

For I went to the stall where they sold sweet lavender.
("Only a penny for a bunch of lavender!")
"Have you got a rabbit, 'cos I don't want lavender?"
   But they hadn't got a rabbit, not anywhere there.

197

I had a penny,
And I had another penny,
I took my pennies
   To the market square.
I did want a rabbit,
A little baby rabbit,
And I looked for rabbits
   'Most everywhere.

And I went to the stall where they sold fresh mackerel.
("Now then! Tuppence for a fresh-caught mackerel!")
"Have you got a rabbit, 'cos I don't like mackerel?"
   But they hadn't got a rabbit, not anywhere there.

I found a sixpence,
A little white sixpence.
I took it in my hand
   To the market square.
I was buying my rabbit
(I do like rabbits),
And I looked for my rabbit
   'Most everywhere.

So I went to the stall where they sold fine saucepans.
("Walk up, walk up, sixpence for a saucepan!")
"Could I have a rabbit, 'cos we've got two saucepans?"
   But they hadn't got a rabbit, not anywhere there.

I had nuffin',
No, I hadn't got nuffin',
So I didn't go down
  To the market square;
But I walked on the common,
The old-gold common . . .
And I saw little rabbits
  'Most everywhere!

So I'm sorry for the people who sell fine saucepans,
I'm sorry for the people who sell fresh mackerel,
I'm sorry for the people who sell sweet lavender,
  'Cos they haven't got a rabbit, not anywhere there!

Daffodowndilly

She wore her yellow sun-bonnet,
　She wore her greenest gown;
She turned to the south wind
　And curtsied up and down.
She turned to the sunlight
　And shook her yellow head,
And whispered to her neighbour:
　"Winter is dead."

Water-Lilies

Where the water-lilies go
To and fro,
Rocking in the ripples of the water,
Lazy on a leaf lies the Lake King's daughter,
And the faint winds shake her.
Who will come and take her?
I will! I will!
Keep still! Keep still!
Sleeping on a leaf lies the Lake King's daughter . . .
Then the wind comes skipping
To the lilies on the water;
And the kind winds wake her.
Now who will take her?
With a laugh she is slipping
Through the lilies on the water.
Wait! Wait!
Too late, too late!
Only the water-lilies go
To and fro,
Dipping, dipping,
To the ripples of the water.

Disobedience

James James
Morrison Morrison
Weatherby George Dupree
Took great
Care of his Mother,
Though he was only three.
James James
Said to his Mother,
"Mother," he said, said he:
"You must never go down to the end of the town,
      if you don't go down with me."

James James
Morrison's Mother
Put on a golden gown,
James James
Morrison's Mother
Drove to the end of the town.
James James
Morrison's Mother
Said to herself, said she:
"I can get right down to the end of the town
      and be back in time for tea."

King John
Put up a notice,
"LOST or STOLEN or STRAYED!
JAMES JAMES
MORRISON'S MOTHER
SEEMS TO HAVE BEEN MISLAID.
LAST SEEN
WANDERING VAGUELY:
QUITE OF HER OWN ACCORD,
SHE TRIED TO GET DOWN TO THE END
OF THE TOWN—FORTY SHILLINGS
REWARD!"

James James
Morrison Morrison
(Commonly known as Jim)
Told his
Other relations
Not to go blaming *him*.
James James
Said to his Mother,
"Mother," he said, said he:
"You must *never* go down to the end of the town
    without consulting me."

James James
Morrison's mother
Hasn't been heard of since.
King John
Said he was sorry,
So did the Queen and Prince.
King John
(Somebody told me)
Said to a man he knew:
"If people go down to the end of the town, well,
    what can *anyone* do?"

(Now then, very softly)

J. J.
M. M.
W. G. Du P.
Took great
C/o his M*****
Though he was only 3.
J. J.
Said to his M*****
"M*****," he said, said he:
"You-must-never-go-down-to-the-end-of-the-town-
    if-you-don't-go-down-with ME!"

Spring Morning

Where am I going? I don't quite know.
Down to the stream where the king-cups grow—
Up on the hill where the pine-trees blow—
Anywhere, anywhere. *I* don't know.

Where am I going? The clouds sail by,
Little ones, baby ones, over the sky.
Where am I going? The shadows pass,
Little ones, baby ones, over the grass.

If you were a cloud, and sailed up there,
You'd sail on water as blue as air,
And you'd see me here in the fields and say:
"Doesn't the sky look green today?"

Where am I going? The high rooks call:
"It's awful fun to be born at all."
Where am I going? The ring-doves coo:
"We do have beautiful things to do."

If you were a bird, and lived on high,
You'd lean on the wind when the wind came by,
You'd say to the wind when it took you away:
"*That's* where I wanted to go today!"

Where am I going? I don't quite know.
What does it matter where people go?
Down to the wood where the blue-bells grow—
Anywhere, anywhere. *I* don't know.

The Island

If I had a ship,
I'd sail my ship,
I'd sail my ship
Through Eastern seas;
Down to a beach where the slow waves
thunder—
The green curls over and the white falls
under—
Boom! Boom! Boom!
On the sun-bright sand.

Then I'd leave my ship and I'd land,
And climb the steep white sand,
And climb to the trees,
The six dark trees,
The coco-nut trees on the cliff's green crown—
Hands and knees
To the coco-nut trees,
Face to the cliff as the stones patter down,
Up, up, up, staggering, stumbling,
Round the corner where the rock is crumbling
Round this shoulder,
Over this boulder,
Up to the top where the six trees stand. . . .

And there would I rest, and lie,
My chin in my hands, and gaze
At the dazzle of sand below,
And the green waves curling slow,
And the grey-blue distant haze
Where the sea goes up to the sky. . . .

And I'd say to myself as I looked so lazily down at
       the sea:
"There's nobody else in the world, and the world
       was made for me."

The Three Foxes

Once upon a time there were three little foxes
Who didn't wear stockings, and they didn't wear
    sockses,
But they all had handkerchiefs to blow their noses,
And they kept their handkerchiefs in cardboard
    boxes.

They lived in the forest in three little houses,
And they didn't wear coats, and they didn't wear
    trousies.
They ran through the woods on their little bare
    tootsies,
And they played "Touch Last" with a family of
    mouses.

They didn't go shopping in the High Street
    shopses,
But caught what they wanted in the woods and
    copses.
They all went fishing, and they caught three
    wormses,
They went out hunting, and they caught three
    wopses.

They went to a Fair, and they all won prizes—
Three plum-puddingses and three mince-pieses.
They rode on elephants and swang on swingses,
And hit three coco-nuts at coco-nut shieses.

That's all that I know of the three little foxes
Who kept their handkerchiefs in cardboard boxes.
They lived in the forest in three little houses,
But they didn't wear coats and they didn't wear
    trousies,
And they didn't wear stockings and they didn't wear
    sockses.

Politeness

If people ask me,
I always tell them:
"Quite well, thank you, I'm very glad to say."
If people ask me,
I always answer,
"Quite well, thank you, how are you today?"
I always answer,
I always tell them,
If they ask me
Politely. . . .
BUT SOMETIMES

I wish

That they wouldn't.

Jonathan Jo

Jonathan Jo
Has a mouth like an "O"
And a wheelbarrow full of surprises;
        If you ask for a bat,
        Or for something like that,
He has got it, whatever the size is.

If you're wanting a ball,
　　It's no trouble at all;
Why, the more that you ask for, the merrier—
　　Like a hoop and a top,
　　And a watch that won't stop,
And some sweets, and an Aberdeen terrier.

Jonathan Jo
　　Has a mouth like an "O"
But this is what makes him so funny:
　　If you give him a smile,
　　Only once in a while,
Then he never expects any money!

At the Zoo

There are lions and roaring tigers, and enormous
   camels and things,
There are biffalo-buffalo-bisons, and a great big
   bear with wings,
There's a sort of a tiny potamus, and a tiny
   nosserus too—
But *I* gave buns to the elephant when *I* went down
   to the Zoo!

There are badgers and bidgers and budgers, and a
    Superintendent's House,
There are masses of goats, and a Polar, and different
    kinds of mouse,
And I think there's a sort of a something which is
    called a wallaboo—
But *I* gave buns to the elephant when *I* went down
    to the Zoo!

If you try to talk to the bison, he never quite
    understands;
You can't shake hands with a mingo—he doesn't
    like shaking hands.
And lions and roaring tigers *hate* saying, "How do
    you do?"—
But *I* give buns to the elephant when *I* go down to
    the Zoo!

Rice Pudding

What is the matter with Mary Jane?
She's crying with all her might and main,
And she won't eat her dinner—rice pudding
     again—
What *is* the matter with Mary Jane?

What is the matter with Mary Jane?
I've promised her dolls and a daisy-chain,
And a book about animals—all in vain—
What *is* the matter with Mary Jane?

What is the matter with Mary Jane?
She's perfectly well, and she hasn't a pain;
But, look at her, now she's beginning again!—
What *is* the matter with Mary Jane?

What is the matter with Mary Jane?
I've promised her sweets and a ride in the train,
And I've begged her to stop for a bit and explain—
What *is* the matter with Mary Jane?

What is the matter with Mary Jane?
She's perfectly well and she hasn't a pain,
And it's lovely rice pudding for dinner again!—
What *is* the matter with Mary Jane?

Missing

Has anybody seen my mouse?

I opened his box for half a minute,
Just to make sure he was really in it,
And while I was looking, he jumped outside!
I tried to catch him, I tried, I tried. . . .
I think he's somewhere about the house.
Has *anyone* seen my mouse?

Uncle John, have you seen my mouse?

Just a small sort of mouse, a dear little brown one,
He came from the country, he wasn't a town one,
So he'll feel all lonely in a London street;
Why, what could he possibly find to eat?

He must be somewhere. I'll ask Aunt Rose:
Have *you* seen a mouse with a woffelly nose?
Oh, somewhere about—
He's just got out. . . .

Hasn't *anybody* seen my mouse?

The King's Breakfast

The King asked
The Queen, and
The Queen asked
The Dairymaid:
"Could we have some butter for
The Royal slice of bread?"
The Queen asked
The Dairymaid,
The Dairymaid
Said, "Certainly,
I'll go and tell
The cow
Now
Before she goes to bed."

The Dairymaid
She curtsied,
And went and told
The Alderney:
"Don't forget the butter for
The Royal slice of bread."

The Alderney
Said sleepily:
"You'd better tell
His Majesty
That many people nowadays
Like marmalade
Instead."

The Dairymaid
Said, "Fancy!"
And went to
Her Majesty.
She curtsied to the Queen, and
She turned a little red:
"Excuse me,
Your Majesty,
For taking of
The liberty,
But marmalade is tasty, if
It's very
Thickly
Spread."

The Queen said
"Oh!"
And went to
His Majesty:
"Talking of the butter for
The Royal slice of bread,
Many people
Think that
Marmalade
Is nicer.
Would you like to try a little
Marmalade
Instead?"

The King said,
"Bother!"
And then he said,
"Oh, dear me!"
The King sobbed, "Oh, deary me!"
And went back to bed.
"Nobody,"
He whimpered,
"Could call me
A fussy man;
I *only* want
A little bit
Of butter for
My bread!"

The Queen said,
"There, there!"
And went to
The Dairymaid.
The Dairymaid
Said, "There, there!"
And went to the shed
The cow said,
"There, there!

I didn't really
Mean it;
Here's milk for his porringer
And butter for his bread."

The Queen took
The butter
And brought it to
His Majesty;
The King said,
"Butter, eh?"
And bounced out of bed.
"Nobody," he said,
As he kissed her
Tenderly,
"Nobody," he said,
As he slid down
The banisters,
"Nobody,
My darling,
Could call me
A fussy man—
BUT
I do like a little bit of butter to my bread!"

Hoppity

Christopher Robin goes
Hoppity, hoppity,

Hoppity, hoppity, hop.
Whenever I tell him
Politely to stop it, he
Says he can't possibly stop.

If he stopped hopping,
       he couldn't go anywhere,
Poor little Christopher
Couldn't go anywhere. . . .
That's why he *always* goes
Hoppity, hoppity,
Hoppity,
Hoppity,
Hop.

At Home

I want a soldier
(A soldier in a busby),
I want a soldier to come and play with me.
I'd give him cream-cakes
(Big ones, sugar ones),
I'd give him cream-cakes and cream for his tea.

I want a soldier
(A tall one, a red one),
I want a soldier who plays on the drum.
Daddy's going to get one
(He's written to the shopman)
Daddy's going to get one as soon as he can come.

The Wrong House

I went into a house, and it wasn't a house,
  It has big steps and a great big hall;
But it hasn't got a garden,
        A garden,
        A garden,
  It isn't like a house at all.

I went into a house, and it wasn't a house,
  It has a big garden and a great high wall;
But it hasn't got a may-tree,
        A may-tree,
        A may-tree,
  It isn't like a house at all.

I went into a house and it wasn't a house—
  Slow white petals from the may-tree fall;
But it hasn't got a blackbird,
        A blackbird,
        A blackbird,
  It isn't like a house at all.

I went into a house, and I thought it was a house,
  I could hear from the may-tree the blackbird
      call. . . .
But nobody listened to it,
        Nobody
        Liked it,
  Nobody wanted it at all.

Summer Afternoon

Six brown cows walk down to drink
  (All the little fishes blew bubbles at the may-fly).
Splash goes the first as he comes to the brink,
  Swish go the tails of the five who follow. . . .
Twelve brown cows bend drinking there
  (All the little fishes went waggle-tail, waggle-tail)—
Six from the water and six from the air;
  Up and down the river darts a blue-black
    swallow.

The Dormouse and the Doctor

There once was a Dormouse who lived in a bed
Of delphiniums (blue) and geraniums (red),
And all the day long he'd a wonderful view
Of geraniums (red) and delphiniums (blue).

A Doctor came hurrying round, and he said:
"Tut-tut, I am sorry to find you in bed.
Just say 'Ninety-nine,' while I look at your
    chest. . . .
Don't you find that chrysanthemums answer the
    best?"

The Dormouse looked round at the view and
   replied
(When he'd said "Ninety-nine") that he'd tried
   and he'd tried,
And much the most answering things that he
   knew
Were geraniums (red) and delphiniums (blue).

The Doctor stood frowning and shaking his head,
And he took up his shiny silk hat as he said:
"What the patient requires is a change," and he
   went
To see some chrysanthemum people in Kent.

The Dormouse lay there, and he gazed at the view
Of geraniums (red) and delphiniums (blue),
And he knew there was nothing he wanted instead
Of delphiniums (blue) and geraniums (red).

The Doctor came back and, to show what he
    meant,
He had brought some chrysanthemum cuttings
    from Kent.
"Now *these*," he remarked, "give a *much* better
    view
Than geraniums (red) and delphiniums (blue)."

They took out their spades and they dug up the
    bed
Of delphiniums (blue) and geraniums (red),
And they planted chrysanthemums (yellow and
    white).
"And *now*," said the Doctor, "we'll *soon* have you
    right."

The Dormouse looked out, and he said with a sigh:
"I suppose all these people know better than I.
It was silly, perhaps, but I *did* like the view
Of geraniums (red) and delphiniums (blue)."

The Doctor came round and examined his chest,
And ordered him Nourishment, Tonics, and Rest,
"How very effective," he said as he shook
The thermometer, "all these chrysanthemums look!"

The Dormouse turned over to shut out the sight
Of the endless chrysanthemums (yellow and white).
"How lovely," he thought, "to be back in a bed
Of delphiniums (blue) and geraniums (red)."

The Doctor said, "Tut! It's another attack!"
And ordered him Milk and Massage-of-the-back,
And Freedom-from-worry and Drives-in-a-car,
And murmured, "How sweet your chrysanthemums
    are!"

The Dormouse lay there with his paws to his eyes
And imagined himself such a pleasant surprise:
"I'll *pretend* the chrysanthemums turn to a bed
Of delphiniums (blue) and geraniums (red)!"

The Doctor next morning was rubbing his hands,
And saying, "There's nobody quite understands
These cases as I do! The cure has begun!
How fresh the chrysanthemums look in the sun!"

The Dormouse lay happy, his eyes were so tight
He could see no chrysanthemums, yellow or white,
And all that he felt at the back of his head
Were delphiniums (blue) and geraniums (red).

And that is the reason (Aunt Emily said)
If a Dormouse gets in a chrysanthemum bed,
You will find (so Aunt Emily says) that he lies
Fast asleep on his front with his paws to his eyes.

Shoes and Stockings

There's a cavern in the mountain
   where the old men meet
(Hammer, hammer, hammer . . .
Hammer, hammer, hammer . . .)
They make gold slippers for my lady's feet
(Hammer, hammer, hammer . . .
Hammer, hammer, hammer . . .)
My lady is marrying her own true knight,
White her gown, and her veil is white,
But she must have slippers on her dainty feet.
Hammer, hammer, hammer . . .
Hammer.

There's a cottage by the river
　where the old wives meet
(Chatter, chatter, chatter . . .
Chatter, chatter, chatter . . .)

They weave gold stockings for my lady's feet
(Chatter, chatter, chatter . . .
Chatter, chatter, chatter . . .)
My lady is going to her own true man,
Youth to youth, since the world began,
But she must have stockings on her dainty feet.
Chatter, chatter, chatter . . .
Chatter.

Sand-Between-the-Toes

I went down to the shouting sea,
Taking Christopher down with me,
For Nurse had given us sixpence each—
And down we went to the beach.

We had sand in the eyes and the ears and
the nose,
And sand in the hair, and sand-between-
the-toes.
Whenever a good nor' wester blows,
Christopher is certain of
Sand-between-the-toes.

The sea was galloping grey and white;
Christopher clutched his sixpence tight;
We clambered over the humping sand—
And Christopher held my hand.

> We had sand in the eyes and the ears and
>   the nose,
> And sand in the hair, and sand-between-
>   the-toes.
> Whenever a good nor' wester blows,
> Christopher is certain of
> Sand-between-the-toes.

There was a roaring in the sky;
The sea-gulls cried as they blew by;
We tried to talk, but had to shout—
Nobody else was out.

> When we got home, we had sand in the hair,
> In the eyes and the ears and everywhere;
> Whenever a good nor' wester blows,
> Christopher is found with
> Sand-between-the-toes.

247

Knights and Ladies

There is in my old picture-book
A page at which I like to look,
Where knights and squires come riding down
The cobbles of some steep old town,
And ladies from beneath the eaves
Flutter their bravest handkerchiefs,
Or, smiling proudly, toss down gages. . . .
But that was in the Middle Ages.
It wouldn't happen now; but still,
Whenever I look up the hill
Where, dark against the green and blue,
The firs come marching, two by two,
I wonder if perhaps I *might*
See suddenly a shining knight
Winding his way from blue to green—
Exactly as it would have been
Those many, many years ago. . . .

Perhaps I might. You never know.

Little Bo-Peep and Little Boy Blue

"What have you done with your sheep,
      Little Bo-Peep?
What have you done with your sheep,
      Bo-Peep?"
"Little Boy Blue, what fun!
I've lost them, every one!"
"Oh, what a thing to have done,
      Little Bo-Peep!"

"What have you done with your sheep,
      Little Boy Blue?
What have you done with your sheep,
      Boy Blue?"
"Little Bo-Peep, my sheep
Went off, when I was asleep."
"I'm sorry about your sheep,
      Little Boy Blue."

"What are you going to do,
          Little Bo-Peep?
What are you going to do,
          Bo-Peep?"
"Little Boy Blue, you'll see
They'll all come home to tea."
"They wouldn't do that for me,
          Little Bo-Peep."

"What are you going to do,
          Little Boy Blue?
What are you going to do,
          Boy Blue?"
"Little Bo-Peep, I'll blow
My horn for an hour or so."
"Isn't that rather slow,
          Little Boy Blue?"

"Whom are you going to marry,
        Little Bo-Peep?
Whom are you going to marry,
        Bo-Peep?"
"Little Boy Blue, Boy Blue,
I'd like to marry you."
"I think I should like it too,
        Little Bo-Peep."

"Where are we going to live,
          Little Boy Blue?
Where are we going to live,
          Boy Blue?"
"Little Bo-Peep, Bo-Peep,
Up in the hills with the sheep."
"And you'll love your little Bo-Peep,
          Little Boy Blue?"

"I'll love you for ever and ever,
          Little Bo-Peep.
I'll love you for ever and ever,
          Bo-Peep."
"Little Boy Blue, my dear,
Keep near, keep very near."
"I shall be always here,
          Little Bo-Peep."

The Mirror

Between the woods the afternoon
Is fallen in a golden swoon,
The sun looks down from quiet skies
To where a quiet water lies,
    And silent trees stoop down to trees.

And there I saw a white swan make
Another white swan in the lake;
And, breast to breast, both motionless,
They waited for the wind's caress . . .
    And all the water was at ease.

253

Halfway Down

Halfway down the stairs
Is a stair
Where I sit.
There isn't any
Other stair
Quite like
It.
I'm not at the bottom,
I'm not at the top;
So this is the stair
Where
I always
Stop.

Halfway up the stairs
Isn't up,
And isn't down.
It isn't in the nursery,
It isn't in the town.
And all sorts of funny thoughts
Run round my head:
"It isn't really
Anywhere!
It's somewhere else
Instead!"

The Invaders

In careless patches through the wood
The clumps of yellow primrose stood,
And sheets of white anemones,
Like driven snow against the trees,
Had covered up the violet,
But left the blue-bell bluer yet.

Along the narrow carpet ride,
With primroses on either side,
Between their shadows and the sun,
The cows came slowly, one by one,
Breathing the early morning air
And leaving it still sweeter there.

And, one by one, intent upon
Their purposes, they followed on
In ordered silence . . . and were gone.

But all the little wood was still,
As if it waited so, until
Some blackbird on an outpost yew,
Watching the slow procession through,
Lifted his yellow beak at last
To whistle that the line had passed. . . .
Then all the wood began to sing
Its morning anthem to the spring.

Before Tea

Emmeline
Has not been seen
For more than a week. She slipped between
The two tall trees at the end of the green. . . .
We all went after her. *"Emmeline!"*

"Emmeline,
I didn't mean—
I only said that your hands weren't clean."
We went to the trees at the end of the green. . . .
But Emmeline
Was not to be seen.

Emmeline
Came slipping between
The two tall trees at the end of the green.
We all ran up to her. "Emmeline!
Where have you been?
Where have you been?
Why, it's more than a week!" And Emmeline
Said, "Sillies, I went and saw the Queen.
She says my hands are *purfickly* clean!"

Teddy Bear

A bear, however hard he tries,
Grows tubby without exercise.
Our Teddy Bear is short and fat
Which is not to be wondered at;
He gets what exercise he can
By falling off the ottoman,
But generally seems to lack
The energy to clamber back.

Now tubbiness is just the thing
Which gets a fellow wondering;
And Teddy worried lots about
The fact that he was rather stout.
He thought: "If only I were thin!
But how does anyone begin?"
He thought: "It really isn't fair
To grudge me exercise and air."

For many weeks he pressed in vain
His nose against the window-pane,
And envied those who walked about
Reducing their unwanted stout.
None of the people he could see
"Is quite" (he said) "as fat as me!"
Then, with a still more moving sigh,
"I mean" (he said) "as fat as I!"

Now Teddy, as was only right,
Slept in the ottoman at night,
And with him crowded in as well
More animals than I can tell;
Not only these, but books and things,
Such as a kind relation brings—
Old tales of "Once upon a time,"
And history retold in rhyme.

One night it happened that he took
A peep at an old picture-book,
Wherein he came across by chance
The picture of a King of France
(A stoutish man) and, down below,
These words: "King Louis So and So,
Nicknamed 'The Handsome'"! There he sat,
And (think of it!) the man was fat!

Our bear rejoiced like anything
To read about this famous King,
Nicknamed "The Handsome." There he sat,
And certainly the man was fat.

Nicknamed "The Handsome." Not a doubt
The man was definitely stout.
Why then, a bear (for all his tub)
Might yet be named "The Handsome Cub"!

"Might yet be named." Or did he mean
That years ago he "might have been"?
For now he felt a slight misgiving:
"Is Louis So and So still living?
Fashions in beauty have a way
Of altering from day to day.
Is 'Handsome Louis' with us yet?
Unfortunately I forget."

Next morning (nose to window-pane)
The doubt occurred to him again.
One question hammered in his head:
"Is he alive or is he dead?"
Thus, nose to pane, he pondered; but
The lattice window, loosely shut,
Swung open. With one startled "Oh!"
Our Teddy disappeared below.

There happened to be passing by
A plump man with a twinkling eye,
Who, seeing Teddy in the street,
Raised him politely to his feet,
And murmured kindly in his ear
Soft words of comfort and of cheer:
"Well, well!" "Allow me!" "Not at all."
"Tut-tut! A very nasty fall."

Our Teddy answered not a word;
It's doubtful if he even heard.
Our bear could only look and look:
The stout man in the picture-book!
That "handsome" King—could this be he,
This man of adiposity?
"Impossible," he thought. "But still,
No harm in asking. Yes I will!"

"Are you," he said, "by any chance
His Majesty the King of France?"
The other answered, "I am that,"
Bowed stiffly, and removed his hat;
Then said, "Excuse me," with an air,
"But is it Mr. Edward Bear?"
And Teddy, bending very low,
Replied politely, "Even so!"

They stood beneath the window there,
The King and Mr. Edward Bear,
And, handsome, if a trifle fat,
Talked carelessly of this and that. . . .
Then said His Majesty, "Well, well,
I must get on," and rang the bell.
"Your bear, I think," he smiled. "Good-day!"
And turned, and went upon his way.

A bear, however hard he tries,
Grows tubby without exercise.
Our Teddy Bear is short and fat,
Which is not to be wondered at.
But do you think it worries him
To know that he is far from slim?
No, just the other way about—
He's *proud* of being short and stout.

Bad Sir Brian Botany

Sir Brian had a battleaxe with great big
    knobs on;
He went among the villagers and blipped them
    on the head.
On Wednesday and on Saturday, but mostly on
    the latter day,
He called at all the cottages, and this is what
    he said:

        "I am Sir Brian!" *(ting-ling)*
        "I am Sir Brian!" *(rat-tat)*
        "I am Sir Brian, as bold as a lion—
           Take *that!*—and *that*—and *that*!"

Sir Brian had a pair of boots with great big spurs
on,
A fighting pair of which he was particularly fond.
On Tuesday and on Friday, just to make the street
look tidy,
He'd collect the passing villagers and kick them in
the pond.
> "I am Sir Brian!" *(sper-lash)*
> "I am Sir Brian!" *(sper-losh!)*
> "I am Sir Brian, as bold as a lion—
> Is anyone else for a wash?"

Sir Brian woke one morning, and he couldn't find
his battleaxe;
He walked into the village in his second pair of
boots.
He had gone a hundred paces, when the street was
full of faces,
And the villagers were round him with ironical
salutes.

"You are Sir Brian? Indeed!
You are Sir Brian? Dear, dear!
You are Sir Brian, as bold as a lion?
Delighted to meet you here!"

Sir Brian went a journey, and he found a lot of
duckweed;

They pulled him out and dried him, and they
blipped him on the head.
They took him by the breeches, and they hurled
him into ditches,
And they pushed him under waterfalls, and this
is what they said:

"You are Sir Brian—don't laugh,
You are Sir Brian—don't cry;
You are Sir Brian, as bold as a lion—
Sir Brian, the lion, good-bye!"

Sir Brian struggled home again, and chopped up
    his battleaxe,
Sir Brian took his fighting boots, and threw them
    in the fire.
He is quite a different person now he hasn't got his
    spurs on,
And he goes about the village as B. Botany, Esquire.

        "I am Sir Brian? Oh, *no!*
         I am Sir Brian? Who's he?
       I haven't got any title, I'm Botany—
        Plain Mr. Botany (B)."

In the Fashion

A lion has a tail and a very fine tail,
And so has an elephant, and so has a whale,
And so has a crocodile, and so has a quail—
    They've all got tails but me.

If I had sixpence I would buy one;
I'd say to the shopman, "Let me try one";
I'd say to the elephant, "This is *my* one."
    They'd all come round to see.

Then I'd say to the lion, "Why, *you've* got a tail!
And so has the elephant, and so has the whale!
And, look! There's a crocodile! *He's* got a tail!
    "You've all got tails like me!"

The Alchemist

There lives an old man at the top of the street,
And the end of his beard reaches down to his feet,
And he's just the one person I'm longing to meet.
    I think that he sounds so exciting;
For he talks all the day to his tortoiseshell cat,
And he asks about this, and explains about that,
And at night he puts on a big wide-awake* hat
    And sits in the writing-room, writing.

He has worked all his life (and he's terribly old)
At a wonderful spell which says, "Lo, and behold!
Your nursery fender is gold!"—and it's gold!
    (Or the tongs, or the rod for the curtain);
But somehow he hasn't got hold of it quite,
Or the liquid you pour on it first isn't right,
So that's why he works at it night after night
    Till he knows he can do it for certain.

* So as not to go to sleep.

Growing Up

I've got shoes with grown up laces,
I've got knickers and a pair of braces,
I'm all ready to run some races.
    Who's coming out with me?

I've got a nice new pair of braces,
I've got shoes with new brown laces,
I know wonderful paddly places.
    Who's coming out with me?

Every morning my new grace is,
"Thank you, God, for my nice braces:
I can tie my new brown laces."
    Who's coming out with me?

If I Were King

I often wish I were a King,
And then I could do anything.

If only I were King of Spain,
I'd take my hat off in the rain.

If only I were King of France,
I wouldn't brush my hair for aunts.

I think, if I were King of Greece,
I'd push things off the mantelpiece.

If I were King of Norroway,
I'd ask an elephant to stay.

If I were King of Babylon,
I'd leave my button gloves undone.

If I were King of Timbuctoo,
I'd think of lovely things to do.

If I were King of anything,
I'd tell the soldiers, "I'm the King!"

Vespers

Little Boy kneels at the foot of the bed,
Droops on the little hands little gold head.
Hush! Hush! Whisper who dares!
Christopher Robin is saying his prayers.

God bless Mummy. I know that's right.
Wasn't it fun in the bath tonight?
The cold's so cold, and the hot's so hot.
Oh! *God bless Daddy*—I quite forgot.

If I open my fingers a little bit more,
I can see Nanny's dressing-gown on the door.
It's a beautiful blue, but it hasn't a hood.
Oh! *God bless Nanny and make her good.*

Mine has a hood, and I lie in bed,
And pull the hood right over my head,
And I shut my eyes, and I curl up small,
And nobody knows that I'm there at all.

Oh! *Thank you, God, for a lovely day.*
And what was the other I had to say?
I said "Bless Daddy," so what can it be?
Oh! Now I remember. *God bless Me.*

Little Boy kneels at the foot of the bed,
Droops on the little hands little gold head.
Hush! Hush! Whisper who dares!
Christopher Robin is saying his prayers.

Word Cloud Classics

Word Cloud Classics

*The Legend of Sleepy Hollow
and Other Tales*

Les Misérables

A Little Princess

Little Women

Love Poems

Mansfield Park

The Merry Adventures of Robin Hood

Moby-Dick

My Ántonia

Mrs. Dalloway

Northanger Abbey

Odyssey

Peter Pan

The Phantom of the Opera

The Picture of Dorian Gray

The Poetry of Emily Dickinson

Presidential Inaugural Addresses

Pride and Prejudice

The Prince and Other Writings

The Prophet and Other Tales

The Romantic Poets

Ruth Bader Ginsburg Dissents

The Scarlet Letter

The Secret Garden

Selected Works of Alexander Hamilton

Selected Works of Edgar Allan Poe

Selected Works of H. G. Wells

Sense and Sensibility

*Strange Case of Dr. Jekyll and
Mr. Hyde & Other Stories*

The Sun Also Rises and Other Stories

A Tale of Two Cities

Tess of the D'Ubervilles

The Three Musketeers

Treasure Island

*Twenty Thousand Leagues
Under the Sea*

*The U.S. Constitution and Other
Key American Writings*

Walden and Civil Disobedience

William Shakespeare Comedies

William Shakespeare Tragedies

*The Wind in the Willows
and Other Stories*

The Wizard of Oz

Wuthering Heights